MW00940889

ROADHOUSE

Sons of Sanctuary MC

Book 5

by

Victoria Danann

THE PLAY LIST

The name of each chapter contains a song on youtube and a video of the lyrics. The songs either set a mood or refer to something specific in the chapter; an event or state of mind.

The songs are almost all classic rock because that is the strong preference of bikers.

This is the first time this feature has been used in my books and I'll be eager to hear what you think. If you care to comment, you're welcome to write me at vdanann@gmail.com.

CHAPTER ONE

HOW'D I END UP HERE?

Rickie Lee Jones – *Night Train*

HOW DID I end up a hundred thousand dollars in credit card debt? It wasn't as hard as it sounds.

I went to Colombia and studied anthropology with a minor in tribal culture. The perfect background to get a great job. Right?

Okay. It was a stupid choice. As it turns out, one of several. But I was still a teenager when I picked a major. I've since learned that brains aren't fully developed until years later. A lot of good that information does me now.

Anyway I graduated with honors and was perfectly prepared for a job at McDonalds across the river in New Jersey. That got me a two bedroom flat in a questionable neighborhood with three roommates who would make most of you run from the building screaming.

Don't pity me. After eight months I parlayed that experience into a job as a bank teller. Sigh. You can pity me a little if you insist.

The point is that, during the last months before graduation, I got dozens of credit card offers in the mail. I said yes to everything. Remember, brain still not fully developed at that point. The result was a hundred thousand dollars' worth of credit.

My thinker may not have been firing on all cylinders yet, but I did know enough to not compound the dismal prospects for my future by adding credit card debt to my school debt, which was already enough to overwhelm Bill Gates.

Of course I made a decision equal to my stunning track record of good choices. I married a cute loser with brown eyes and hair that fell over his forehead in a dreamy way. Six months later he left me for a skank ho. Shortly thereafter, I had a divorce that was very much wanted and a surprise that was very much unwanted. He'd left me with a hundred thousand dollar credit card debt.

Yeah. He'd been getting to the mail first and hiding the notices. Let me tell you. Ignorance is only bliss if you're blind to things that can't hurt you. If you're blind to things that *can* hurt you, you're not a Pollyanna goofball. You're an idiot.

I may have been contemplating suicide when I opened my gym locker and found a really cute Bed Stu zip tote with two hundred and seventy-five thousand dollars in it. I looked around to see if it was a joke. Or a bad spy cam TV show.

Of course I didn't know exactly how much money was in there at the time. I wasn't going to count it while standing there. What I was going to do was maintain my stellar record of always picking the worst option. Because I may be well-educated, but I'm an idiot. I quietly pulled the tote straps over my shoulder and walked out.

Well, what would you do?

After counting out the money in the bathroom, the only place where I can find privacy these days, I lowered the toilet seat cover, sat down, and decided that if the gods had seen fit to give me a second chance, I wouldn't be dumb with it. Again.

I was scheduled to start work at nine. I got ready for the day and walked the two blocks to work like every other day. Except that day I had a large, alright huge, cash deposit. In a gym bag.

If I'd tried to conduct such a transaction as a customer there would have been many questions accompanied with raised eyebrows. But I wasn't a customer. I was an employee. I should mention that it was also an ideal day. Wednesday.

I knew there would be sometime during the day when I would be the only person at the counter. The drive-through would be dead. The other teller would be on lunch. The manager would be in the corner office. The "personal bankers" would be at their desks in the front of the building and wouldn't be able to see what was happening behind the glass even if they'd cared.

Of course it would be on camera, but no one would ever see the feed unless I was unlucky enough to deposit all that money on the same day the bank was robbed. I figured my spell of unluck had just taken a major turn for the better. I had a rich secret admirer who could pick a lock and wanted absolutely nothing in return for a whole lot of cash.

I pulled it off.

The money was in my account for less than a couple of hours before it had paid off credit cards and student loans.

I was free.

Until the rightful owners of the money, who wanted it back, traced the hasty stash to my locker. I learned this during a very scary conversation in the restroom at Starbucks. Just as I was about to close and lock the unisex door behind me, two guys with dark hair, dark eyes, ill-fitting suits and eyebrows that met in the middle stepped inside, shushing me as they did.

I took a big lungful of air to scream, but number two goon grabbed me from behind and clamped his sweaty palm over my mouth. Did I mention it smelled like week-old garlic press? Ugh.

While I was wondering if the man was a cook masquerading as a thug, the other one said, "Where's the money, Clover?"

Oh, god, they know my name.

I shook my head, meaning that I couldn't talk with number two goon's hand over my mouth. He thought I meant that I was refusing to tell him.

"Don't even think about telling me you don't know where it is."

I didn't shake my head, but tried to talk against, retch, garlic hand. Apparently he got the message. His attention flicked to my captor. When he nodded, I was released just enough to speak.

"I do know where it is. Part of it is in the banks that sponsor my credit cards. The rest is in the U.S. Treasury Department of Student Loans."

Goon number one's eyes narrowed in a way that would have been much more chilling if I hadn't known that, just on the other side of the door down a short hallway there were twenty-five people ordering coffee and sipping such concoctions as venti cinnamon lattes with a splash of classic syrup and a dribble of caramel sauce while five baristas dashed around trying to keep up.

"That's not good news for you." He waited for me to say something. I didn't. "Here's the thing, doll. We know who you are. Obviously. We know where you are. Obviously. And the fella I work for wants his money back."

After a lengthy uncomfortable stare, I said, "You want me to get the money back."

His mouth twitched ever so slightly.

I suppose he was talking to goon number two when he said, "She's quick, this one."

Goon number two chuckled in a way that caused fear to begin building. There was something dark in his laugh. It creeped me out in ways that required an expanded imagination and adequately conveyed the urgency of finding a way to appease.

"I can get it."

"You can?" number one said slowly.

I nodded enthusiastically. "Yes. I just need, um, six

years?"

That got me another lip twitch. "Funny." He looked over my shoulder again. "She's funny. Right?" Goon number two repeated that low laugh that made goosebumps break out, not the good kind. "I was thinking more along the lines of six hours."

"Hours?" I squeaked.

Goon number one studied me for a minute. "Look. You're cute and we're reasonable guys. We're gonna give you three days. Till Saturday night. If you have the money, we'll call it square even though you've caused some trouble."

"I've caused some trouble? I didn't put that bag in my gym locker."

Goon number one lowered his chin and gave me a menacing look. "Maybe not. But you knew it wasn't yours."

"Did you want me to turn it into Lost and Found?"

He pressed his lips together. "Saturday night. No matter where you are. No matter who you're with. If you don't have the money, you're going to work for our organization." His eyes drifted up and down my body slowly as goon number two's hands drifted up and down my body slowly. I took in a horrified breath when he grabbed private girl parts. "And I figure you'll work it off in about sixteen years."

Shit!

Goon number two released me abruptly as they both stepped toward the door. "Don't worry about contact. We'll find you." Goon number two opened the door. Goon number one looked back over his shoulder. "Get the money."

My first thought was… *I can't get the money.*

My second thought was to go home and review my options.

My third thought was to run.

I went with my third thought.

This is the story of what happened after that fateful decision.

CHAPTER TWO

RESURRECTION

John Mellencamp – *Paper In Fire*

Seven Months Ago

H E BARELY REMEMBERED his real name. He'd been called Raze since long before puberty. Partly, no doubt, because of his last name. Rouen was French but somewhere along the way his people had given up and started pronouncing it like "ruin". The other part of the reason was based on behavior. He'd like to say he didn't deserve it, but Raze had been the hellraising sort.

Memory was fuzzy as to whether he'd been kicked out of school or had left on his own, but the fact was that after football season was over his senior year, there just hadn't been a good reason to stay. It wasn't like he'd been shiftless. He had a job at his uncle's auto repair and his uncle appreciated him a hell of a lot more than the high school did.

Raze's mother had died when he was ten. His dad had moved them in with his Uncle Farrell and then just left one night. No goodbyes. No reasons. If Uncle Farrell, a dedicated bachelor, felt burdened being left with an abandoned nephew, he never let on.

Raze got full pay on the condition that he spend two hours a day reading. So every day between twelve and two, Raze sat at the vinyl top kitchen table in his uncle's kitchen and read the books put in front of him. He would've liked to cheat, but he had to answer questions about what he'd read while he was working on cars in the afternoon. Philosophy, which was useless. History, which Raze had to admit wasn't *entirely* useless. A little literature, some of which was okay. Jack Kerouac yes. Tolstoy no.

Truthfully he learned more in the months after dropping out than he had in the whole of high school to that point. And since he had the job he wanted, there was no downside.

Later he got his GED so that he could join the National Guard.

Long story made short. A short few years later, he found himself with a young wife who wanted more than a head mechanic's paycheck could offer. He was young, stupid and down with doing his best to make his bride happy. So when she suggested he could generate a few extra bucks by joining the Guard, he reluctantly agreed. He figured he wouldn't mind helping out with a natural disaster. If something like that happened, he'd help without getting paid. But life takes unexpected turns sometimes.

He ended up deployed to Afghanistan as a driver for a med unit. In a combat zone. While he was plunged dick-deep into hell, young Mrs. Rouen moved in with the guy who took Raze's place at the auto shop.

And he had to learn about it from his uncle. "Sorry to lay it on you like this, but thought you had to know."

After two deployments, Raze came home bitter, divorced, wearing a permanent scowl between his brows and wanting nothing more to do with the auto repair.

Farrell Rouen died a few weeks before Raze came home. He'd inherited the auto repair, the house that he'd more or less grown up in, and nine hundred thousand dollars. That was a shock. Nobody would have ever guessed Uncle Farrell was sitting on a bucket of cash.

He sold everything in the auto repair, cleaned out the house except for his own bedroom furniture and keepsakes, repainted, and bought new furniture. He also cleaned out the studio apartment his uncle had built behind the garage when he and Becky had gotten married so they didn't have to share the house with him and stored his personal things in there.

Stuff sorted out, he settled into his mission. He planned to spend some years getting serious with a bottle. A few weeks into that plan, things were going well. At least if self-destruction was the goal.

Sitting at the new dinette table, he heard the rumbling of a Harley. He didn't have to look out the window to know who it was. He'd played football with Brash Fornight in high school and they'd been tight. Right up until his marriage. Looking back, he could see that Brash hadn't enjoyed being around Becky.

Raze didn't have a cell phone and didn't want one, but he hadn't taken out the land line that had been in his uncle's house practically since phones were invented. Brash had called twice a week and left messages, each one advising that Raze should change the greeting on the voicemail service. Raze knew what Brash said on the messages because he listened to them. Every one. He didn't pick up the phone because he didn't want to talk, but he was oddly compelled to listen to voicemail.

Apparently Brash had gotten tired of waiting for a reply and decided to communicate the old school way. Face to face.

When the bike shut off, Raze shuffled to the screen door and pushed it open. Brash walked in without a word, but absorbed a world of information as he walked by Raze and sat down at the kitchen table. Still without speaking, Raze set a glass in front of Brash and poured two fingers of the not-so-special whiskey he was drinking.

SILENCE CONTINUED FOR about fifteen minutes. Finally Raze said, "I guess you're bein' nosy."

"If that's what you call it when friends give a damn about you." Raze sighed. "Heard about Becky."

Raze stared at his glass. "Yeah."

"Sorry about your uncle."

"Yeah."

"I don't remember this kitchen bein' so... gray."

"Had it redone."

"Huh." Brash wondered if his friend was color-blind because everything in the kitchen was gray. Walls, ceiling, counters, cabinets, appliances, floor. "What are you gonna do with..." Brash halfheartedly waved his glass in the direction of the auto shop, "...the place?"

"Don't know yet."

"Alright. Well. While you're thinkin' on it, why don't you come on over to the clubhouse? Say hello. Have a drink with friends. Gettin' out could only do you good."

"Sure. Sometime soon."

In a demonstration worthy of his earned nickname,

Brash slammed his palm down on the table, making the bottle rattle, and bared his teeth. "NOW!"

Raze didn't startle. He slowly slid his eyes to Brash. "Some. Time. Soon."

Brash didn't want a confrontation with Raze, but he thought he'd been left alone long enough. "Put it this way. Come with me. Or I'll show up with the club and we'll all have a drink here."

"Thanks for the warning. I'll be armed."

As Raze reached for the bottle to punctuate the idea that the conversation was over, Brash swiped it out of reach. Before Raze could form a proper objection, Brash had walked to the sink and emptied it.

"I'm givin' you a choice clear and simple." He leaned back against the sink and crossed his arms. "Sons. Or rehab."

Raze stared dumbfounded for a few seconds, his mind trying to make sense of how those two very dissimilar things formed options in Brash's mind. "What makes you think I won't run your trespassin' asses off the property with a shotgun?"

Brash's lips twitched in amusement before lazily spreading into a smile. "I heard war changes people. But not *that* much."

Raze mulled that over and had to admit it was true. If the club showed up and stormed his little screen door, he wasn't sure what he'd do, but he wouldn't shoot at them. "Yeah? Maybe I'll just call the sheriff."

Brash's smile gave way to laughter. "Uh-huh. Blake would probably laugh harder than I just did if you called him up and said, 'Help. The Sons are here to try and stop me from drinkin' myself to death and becomin' a waste of life'."

Raze sat back in his chair. "That's harsh. Even for you."

Brash got quiet. "I wish it was overly critical. Sadly. It's true."

"I'm just takin' some time to think things through."

"Uh-huh. Well. Time's up." Brash looked toward the shop. "Your ride still runnin'?"

"Don't know. Don't care."

"That so? 'Cause when I peeked through the shop

door window I could see that the place has been cleaned up. Everything's been cleared out except for…"

"I know my own goddamned inventory, Brash. Christ. What is it you're after?"

Brash pulled the coffee pot out, filled it with water, and started looking through the cupboards for coffee.

"You should get one of those pod machines. We got one over at the club. Real handy for when you just need one or two cups quick."

It wasn't lost on Raze that Brash had ignored his question. "Might as well stop right there 'cause I'm not drinkin' that stuff."

"I can't let you get on your bike in a condition of advanced inebriation."

"Advanced inebriation? Who talks like that?"

Brash shrugged. "My wife." He turned to Raze, realizing he'd married while Raze was away. "You should meet her. She's really somethin'."

"Yeah. Congratulations." The word was thick with sarcasm.

"Thanks." Brash hesitated with spoon in midair before continuing to scoop extra big helpings of coffee into the paper filter.

When he finished and started the machine, Raze spoke up. "I'm not havin' any of that. So I hope you're in the mood for a half gallon of coffee. And you did not tell me what you're after." Swiping a hand through his hair in a show of exasperation, he said, "Why are you even here?"

Brash's features softened. He sat down at the table again and for a couple of minutes there was no sound in the room except for Mr. Coffee's inappropriately cheerful gurgle.

"You remember that time… when we played those rich kids at Leander?"

Brash figured the look on Raze's face was as close as the man could get to a smile in the current version of himself. "I do."

Brash laughed. "Man, were we outmatched. In every way possible. I got laid out like a corpse by a monster, six four and three hundred pounds. He was supposed to be a kid, but I've always had my doubts. I get back twinges somethin' awful when the barometric pressure drops." Brash glanced at Raze to make sure he was following. "I know what you're thinkin'. The wife says I have to make a choice between Texas and medicinal cannabis. She has visions of goin' to the house for weed." He chuckled. "I tease her by sayin' it would give her bar street cred. She doesn't find that as funny as I do. Way I see it… it's a plant for Christ's sake. And the Creator didn't say you can eat these plants, but not those."

Raze grunted agreement.

"Anyhow. I'm on the ground like a rag doll. I knew better than to move. Truthfully, I was just concentratin' on tryin' not to bawl like a baby in front of my friends. Not to mention girls.

"People started runnin' at me from the home side-line. Medics. Trainer. My old man." He glanced at Raze again. "But before any of 'em got to me, you were down on the ground on your knees leanin' close and sayin', 'I'll get him for you, Brannach'." Brash stopped to smile. "I had no idea you knew my real name. Didn't know *anybody* knew my real name except the people with the keys to the file cabinets in the office.

"So they put me on a stretcher and carried me off to the side, but they started the clock again when they were loadin' my ass onto the ambulance. I turned my head even though they'd told me not to. Sure 'nough. That fucker was laid out same as me. You standin' there with a big grin, givin' me a thumbs up.

"Don't know how you did it. You're no bigger than me." The coffee maker announced with an extended hiss that it had discharged its duty. Brash got up, poured a mug full, and set it down in front of Raze. "Not the kind of thing I'm likely to forget."

Raze cleared his throat. "Look, Brash. You don't owe..."

"Shut up and drink that down." He nodded to keys on a holder near the door. "Those the keys to the shop?"

Raze narrowed his eyes. "Why?"

Brash didn't wait for his answer. He pulled the key ring off the cup hook and started for the door. "Gonna see if your ride is up for a spin."

Raze huffed. "I told you…"

"Heard you, Ruin." Brash walked out without looking back.

Two hours later Raze was more sober than he'd been since he'd been back, which was a good thing because he was speeding along beside Brash Fornight, the deafening rumble of Harleys filling a place in his heart he hadn't realized was empty and yearning. It wasn't lost on him that there was probably a reason why he'd scraped off almost everything in his life that was tangible, but kept the bike. He'd even done a little maintenance to make sure it was good as gold, but he hadn't taken it out.

Until Brash came for him.

The feel of evening air rushing past was like an elixir moving slowly through his veins to rearrange his molecules and give him a reason, that single elusive reason that had been successfully evading him, to think life might still have something for him. The other bike keeping pace with him, a steady reminder that he wasn't as alone as he'd thought, began to heal the frayed edges of his soul.

"GOT A GUEST, boys," Brash announced as he stepped into the clubhouse kitchen a step ahead of Raze.

Raze got a hearty welcome from club members who were also there for supper.

There was a time, when Brash had prospected, that Raze had considered club life, but had decided to go another way. There was an unspoken feeling in the club that he could have been, would have been, one of them if he'd chosen it. That and his relationship with Brash made him an honorary of sorts, a friend of the club. More than a 'hang around'. But not an official member.

After dinner with the seven people who showed for food and easy conversation, they adjourned to the bar.

"Don't you have a wife to get home to?" Raze asked Brash.

Brash shook his head. "She's gone to Houston for a shoppin' trip. It's the semiannual drain-the-bank-account girls' thing organized by my mother."

A single barked laugh escaped Raze's chest and

shook his body in a way that was alien and called attention to itself. He realized he hadn't laughed in a long, long time. So long his body was reacting like it wasn't sure that was normal.

He was just about to tell the recruit behind the bar that he'd have whiskey, but Brash beat him to it. Brash had gone around the bar, pulled two long necks out of ice and set a cold beer in front of Raze. The look he gave Brash was part glare, part amusement, part admiration, and part affection. He took the beer and pulled down a long swig. Brash took a stool next to him and did the same while studying his friend.

"You're staring," Raze said quietly.

"Yeah."

"I'm not suicidal if that's what you're thinkin'."

"So happens that's *not* what I'm thinkin'."

Raze lifted his chin and gave Brash a ghost of a smile. "There's something you're itchin' to share. And I think I'd rather hear it than continue the silent examination."

"Why didn't you return my calls?"

"Didn't want to talk."

Brash exhaled a long weary-sounding breath. "Why's that?"

"I'm thinkin' I'm not the best company right now."

"Why's that?"

Raze turned to look Brash in the face. "My troubles are my own."

"And there it is."

"What's that supposed to mean?"

"Means you're dead wrong. Means so long as you got people who care about you, your troubles are not *just* yours."

Raze took a gulp of his beer and glanced around the room before answering. "I hear what you're sayin'. And it means somethin' to me. A lot, actually. But…"

"If the next thing you're gonna say is that you need to hole up and nurse your wounds with Jack Daniels, I'm gonna say that's unacceptable."

Raze almost smiled. Brash's audaciousness was one of the things he'd always liked about the biker kid. He supposed that was the reason why he'd earned the nickname Brash.

"Well, the thing is, for good or bad, it's not up to you."

"Makin' it up to me."

At that Raze felt a chuckle bubble up in his throat. His friend was clearly on a mission to rescue him and he knew Brash well enough to know that Raze represented the bone he'd taken hold of. He wasn't going to let go until the world was leveled.

"So you're out to save me, are you?" Raze didn't try to disguise his amusement. The idea was preposterous.

He'd ended up in a horror of a war because of a woman who wanted more shoes. While he was in the middle of that, she'd betrayed him, and the only family he had left had died. He felt like he was more than entitled to a few decades of alcoholic oblivion.

The question was rhetorical. So Brash didn't answer.

"How're you gonna do that?"

"Gonna help you find your way to somethin' useful."

"Somethin' useful," Raze repeated drily.

"That's right. Your mind's full of dark thoughts. Can't do anything about that. Can't change what you've been through. But we can give you something to do until some other thoughts start fillin' up your pail."

"I don't wanna be your project, Brash."

"Too bad. Here's the thing. The club has interests that are far-reaching. Probably more so than anybody not involved with the day-to-day would guess. If you added in my brother's business, well, you'd know the Fornights have forks in a whole damn lot of pies."

When Brash stopped talking, Raze said, "If that has something to do with me, I'm not makin' the connection."

Brash paused, like he was trying to feel out what to say next. Careful wasn't his modus operandi, but he could tread softer when he needed to.

"D'you know my pop started out as a hands-on mechanic?"

That seemed to catch Raze's interest. "No."

Brash grinned. "He was so damn good he was head

mechanic for The Yellow Rose when he was still in his twenties."

"I did not know that."

Brash chuckled. "Yeah. The custom business grew outta that."

"Huh."

"The point I'm gettin' to is this."

"Finally."

"Hear me out. I'm tryin' to say that life's a path with twists and turns. Sometimes we don't know what's around the next bend. Might be bad. Might be good. But as long as we keep gettin' up every day we're gonna find out. What do you think I do?"

"Do?"

"Yes. Do. What do you think I do with my time?" It was clear that Raze didn't have a ready answer. "I'm guessin' by the silence and the blank look on your face that you have no clue."

"Sorry to say I got no clue. I guess that makes me a self-involved son of a bitch."

"Let's not stray from the point at hand. Which is

that I finance and supervise entrepreneurial businesses."

"No shit."

Brash nodded. "Hard as it might be to believe, it's a fact. Got little money makers humming away all over town. Dry cleaners. Stainless steel fabricators. Delis. Outdoor kitchens. Pool supplies. Taco stands. I could go on, but you get the picture."

"That's... kinda impressive." Raze looked and sounded sincerely impressed. "All legit?"

That caused Brash to lean back a bit. "Yes. What'd you think? That we're an outlaw club?"

"Well..."

"Is that why you didn't throw in with us? You thought we were..." Raze didn't answer. "Well, to be fair. Things may not have been entirely up and up in my granddad's day. But Pop changed all that after I was born."

Raze nodded slightly. "Meant no offense."

"None taken." Brash shoved his empty bottle toward the inner edge of the bar. "This is what I want to know. If you could spend your days doin' something besides sittin' in your kitchen with a bottle, what would it be? I get that sellin' off your tools means you're not wantin' to reopen the auto repair." Raze looked at Brash, but said nothing as he finished off his beer. Brash took that as agreement. "So. If it's not that, then what is it?"

"What is what?"

"Don't play dumb with me. I know better." Brash knocked on the bar. The prospect hurried over. "Coffee. Two." He turned back to Raze. "If you were goin' to do somethin' with your days besides sittin' in your kitchen with Jack Daniels, what would it be?"

One question.

One simple, straightforward question was all it took.

An image danced across Raze's inner field of vision of a night when he'd been on the road that followed the Guadalupe River just outside Kerrville. It was about nine o'clock and just a little over an hour from home. He'd made an easy turn and come up on an ice house. It was a nice night so the bay doors were open and he could see inside. Band playing. People at the bar. Sitting at picnic tables inside and out. Bikes parked in a row off to one side of pickups and cars.

He pulled in and switched off the ignition. He sat on the bike for a few minutes just taking it in. The lights. The music. The laughter. It was inviting. Welcoming. The essence of aliveness housed in a place called The Lupe.

Raze kept that to himself.

"Don't know," he lied.

"Alright. Consider the seed planted. Now I want you to stay overnight 'cause I got somethin' to show you in the mornin'."

Raze was shaking his head. "Nope. Thanks for the invitation, but I'm getting' back home."

"Got a guest room right down the hall with a new toothbrush and clean sheets. Stay tonight."

"Brash. Read my lips. I'm goin' home."

"No, you're not."

Raze almost laughed. "Who's gonna stop me?"

"Well, technically nobody's gonna stop you, but if you go you're walkin', because your bike keys have gone missin'. And…" Brash turned a shit-eating grin his way, "you can't call Uber 'cause you don't have a phone."

Raze sat back looking incredulous. The move was far out of line. Even for Brash. "You're plannin' to hold me captive."

"Of course not," Brash said in the most serious tone. "We're gonna offer our very fine hospitality while we're lookin' for your keys." His smile returned. "I'm sure we'll find them by mid-morning."

"Fuck," Raze muttered.

"Meantime, you can hang out here. Play some pool. Get to know your friends again." Brash gave him a meaningful look. "And think about what I said."

Raze wanted to be mad. He thought he should be mad. But he wasn't mad. For the first time in forever he felt himself take in a breath that went all the way to the bottom of his lungs.

It was clear that Brash had made a success of an entrepreneurial empire with force of will and an absolute unwavering certainty that, once he'd made up his mind, he was right and not taking no for an answer.

Raze respected that. For less than a second he thought about walking home, to save his pride, but decided that was ridiculous. Brash had something going on in his head. Raze was more than a little curious to see what it was, so he decided he was going to let it play out.

"If you stay on tomorrow night, which happens to be Friday, there'll be girls here. Single. Willing," Brash said with eyebrows raised.

"Girls," he repeated with derision. "I'll be gone by… ten did you say? I've had enough of girls."

"You got a bad one. There's no denyin' that. But they're not all…"

"Save it."

Brash held up his hands in surrender. "Not my business."

Raze barked out a laugh. "Oh! *That's* not your business, but everything else about my life is."

Ignoring the sarcasm, Brash agreed with Raze's assessment. "We see eye to eye. That's exactly how I'm thinkin' of it, too."

CHAPTER THREE

RAZE & RUIN

The Doors – *Roadhouse Blues*

L IGHT WAS STREAMING through the high rectangular windows when Raze woke up. He had to admit that he'd gone for several hours without dwelling on Becky or the war or the fact that he hadn't been able to get home in time for his uncle's funeral. He also felt something he thought he would never feel again. Gratitude.

He hadn't slept well. Not because the set up wasn't comfortable. The sheets were new. The air conditioning was just right. The walls that had been separated by concrete blocks and insulated were virtually sound-proof. And it wasn't because he hadn't been tired enough to sleep. He had been.

It was because he hadn't been able to get that image of the ice house out of his head. The last thing he'd ever thought he would do in this life was own a bar. Or a restaurant. Or a music club. But he'd spent a night tossing and turning while considering taking on all three at once.

Sometime in the wee hours after he'd made a decision, whether he realized it, or admitted it, or not, he drifted off.

There was a fairly tight seal on the guest room door, but unless his mind was playing tricks, he smelled bacon. He loved bacon. That inner acknowledgement led him to ask himself why he didn't cook more. It wasn't like he didn't know how to fry bacon.

He glanced at the bedside clock, which might or might not be right. Eight thirteen. There was no way to verify that because he didn't wear a watch, but it felt close to right.

As promised there was a new, still in the package toothbrush in the drawer next to the sink. Shampoo. Soap. No comb, but that was what fingers were for.

He stripped down. Got clean and put his clothes back on, minus the underwear that was unceremoniously dumped in the trash. It wouldn't hurt him to go commando for a few hours.

When he stepped out into the hall he was alone, but heard faint sounds of dish clanking and the murmur of conversation.

Eric looked up from the remains of eggs, pancakes, and bacon. "You just made it, sleepy. Kitchen closes at nine on weekdays."

"You run a tight schedule for bikers," Raze answered.

"What'll you have?" said the cook.

Raze pointed at Eric's plate. "I'll have what he's havin' if that's okay."

"Comin' up," she said with an authority that implied that nothing, not earthquake, hurricane or flood could prevent Raze from being presented with perfectly prepared eggs, bacon, and pancakes.

Brash was sitting at the end of the table with the Austin American-Statesman spread out in front of him and a coffee mug in his hand. He nodded at Raze and kicked out the chair next to him, which was biker for, "Sit here."

Raze spoke to Arnold on the way to the end of the table. To Brash he said, "Thought only old people read papers."

"Make of it what you will," Brash replied good-naturedly, implying that it would be near to impossible to ruffle him.

"So where's my surprise?"

Brash grinned. "Glad you're greetin' the morning with a spark of eagerness."

"I wouldn't go that far." When Brash still didn't answer the question, he said, "Let me guess. There's not really somethin' you want to show me."

"Oh. There is. There definitely is. Let's finish up breakfast. Then we'll head out."

"So you found my keys?"

"Nope." Brash shook his head. "We're walkin'."

Cook set a cup of coffee down in front of Raze.

He looked up. "Thanks."

"Want anything in it?" she said.

"No. It's good," Raze answered.

She nodded her approval. "Black. That's the way real men drink their coffee." She looked at Eric pointedly in reference to the teasing she regularly gave him about excessive sugar and cream.

"Hey," Eric said. "It's your job to serve the coffee. Any way we want it. Not to comment on how we like it."

"Nobody's talkin' to you, Eric," she returned.

Eric rolled his eyes in exasperation, looking more like a perplexed middle schooler than a seasoned biker.

Raze could see he wasn't getting any more out of Brash. So he decided to take a section of the paper, drink his coffee, eat his breakfast, and wait.

When he shoveled the last forkful of eggs in his mouth, Brash said, "You ready?"

Raze took a swallow of coffee and nodded.

He followed Brash out the front door, but instead of heading toward the hangar where they did maintenance and kept the bikes parked, or the parking lot where they kept the enclosed vehicles, they turned left. It had been years since he'd been to the compound and, clearly, things had changed. For one, there were more buildings. Like the metal warehouse they were walking towards.

When they got closer, Raze thought he heard barking.

Brash opened the door and held it for Raze to enter the front room that seemed to be set up as an office. There was a large desk with a computer and two brown leather Chesterfields. The walls were covered with photos of German Shepherds and families loving on them.

After Brash pushed the button on the wall that looked like a doorbell, it only took a minute for a face to appear at the porthole in the door. The guy nodded and disappeared.

"What is this?" Raze asked.

"One of our businesses. We raise the best family security dogs in the world."

Raze opened his mouth to say something about

that, but before he got it out the inner door opened and the guy from the porthole stepped in with a dog on a leash.

"This is Rescue," Brash said by way of introduction.

"You mean a rescue dog?" Raze asked carefully.

"No," Brash chuckled. "This…" he pointed, "is Rescue. This…" he pointed at the dog, "is Bless."

Bless looked up at Raze and tilted her head like she was waiting for him to say or do something.

"Hello," he said to the dog.

Rescue let go of the leash and Bless padded toward Raze. She sat down in front of him and lifted a paw. He took her paw and, without giving it any thought, got down on his knees. Bless reached out and gave his chin a tentative lick. He reached out and ran his hand down the fur of her neck and shoulder.

Then a most shocking and inexplicable thing occurred. Raze, who hadn't cried since he'd gotten a broken wrist at age seven, began to blink back a stinging sensation in his eyes. At the same time his throat felt thick enough to prevent a swallow.

When Brash sensed the heaviness of intense emotion spiking in the room, he signaled to Rescue to follow him outside. On some level Raze was aware that he'd been left alone with the dog. As if she understood the crucial role she had to play in the stranger's journey, Bless sat quietly and absorbed Raze's pain as silent tears overflowed.

After wiping his face with his shirt sleeves, he looked at the dog like she was a miracle. "You got some special stuff?" he asked her. She licked his chin again. "Yeah. You got some special stuff. A couple of hours ago I would have said I'm not a man who talks to dogs."

When he began to feel the press of the hard floor on his knees, he got up and sat down on one of the Chesterfields. Bless followed, sat, and rested her head on his knee, ears forward as if asking for more attention.

When Brash and Rescue returned, Raze looked up and said simply, "I want this dog."

Brash smiled. "Looks like she might be amenable to that."

"I don't care how much she costs."

"She's not for sale. She's yours, but we retain part ownership. She's a breeder. You bring her back when she's in heat. Then put up with puppies for a few weeks. She's not your kind of ordinary dog. Her real name is…"

He looked to Rescue, who said, "Bleggherstein's Kronprinzessin."

Brash nodded. "We call her Bless for obvious reasons."

Raze looked at Brash with a light in his eye that hadn't been there before. "Puppies." He looked at the dog. "I can do that."

"There's two more conditions. And we insist on this for all the dogs. So it's not just you being singled out. You spend three days here learning everything there is to know about this dog, her care, her training, and how to handle her. Canine psychology. That sort of thing. It's basically training for you."

"You have people stay in the clubhouse?"

"No. That cottage? Maybe you didn't notice it. There's a two bedroom cottage on the path where new families stay. You can be there or in the clubhouse. Up to you."

"What's the other condition?"

"You have to use our vet. She gets heartworm and flea-tick meds once a month. Shots every six months. Anything happens, you call her."

"Okay. I need to go home and get some clothes."

"Sure. This will also give us three days to talk about what you're gonna do with your life. Besides being the proud owner of one of our dogs."

When he started to get up, Bless automatically jumped down.

"I'll be back," he told the dog.

She responded with ears pricked and a small wag of the tail.

Brash reached into his pocket and withdrew the keys to Raze's bike. "Well, lookie here. What d'ya know? I guess they were right there all along."

Raze gave him a look as he took his keys. "You busy?"

Brash looked momentarily stunned by the question.

He hadn't been expecting Raze to reach out. According to Brigid's friends who knew about such things, he'd thought that, if there was an indication of an interest in rejoining the living, it wouldn't happen for a while. He'd committed to the long haul and accepted that things might not end well for his friend.

"I'm never too busy for you," was Brash's solemn reply.

Raze took in a deep breath. "Ride home with me? Somethin' I want to ask about."

Brash nodded. "Give me five minutes." He kept an actual office with an actual secretary and went there as little as possible. Beatrice, his right hand woman, made that possible and he adored her for it. She kept track of every detail of a network of businesses that was complicated to say the very least and she made it look easy.

"Fornight," she answered simply.

"It's me."

"Morning, sir."

"You do not have to call me sir, Bea."

"I do. Yes. I do. Your mother says it's dignified and

promotes a professional atmosphere."

"You work for a biker, Bea. How professional do you think the 'atmosphere' needs to be? Especially since you're the only person in the office ninety-eight percent of the time?"

"I take your point, sir. But I have no intention of going up against your mama. 'Bout anything."

He sighed, fully grasping the wisdom of that and conceded the point for the time being. "Yeah. You and me both." But he made a mental note to instruct his mother to leave his secretary the hell alone. "Callin' because I'm gonna be out of pocket for a few hours. You can reach me in case of emergency, but you need to rearrange my schedule. I think I was supposed to stop by four or five shops today?"

"Five. So you'll be out all day?"

"Can't say, but I think it's best if we plan on it. I can work this weekend, so shift my stops to the folks who are open Saturday or Sunday."

"Your wife will be back Sunday."

"Saturday then."

"I'll do my best, sir."

"You tryin' to get my goat, Bea?"

He heard a womanly giggle. "Take it up with your mother. Sir. She's also instructed me to 'dress for success'. So I'll be needin' a raise to cover wardrobe."

He hung up while muttering, "For Christ's sake."

RAZE WAS LEANING over the open hood of a 1967 Camaro in deep dialogue with a transfer named Press who Brant thought was as capable with machinery as anybody he'd ever seen.

"I'm good to go," yelled Brash.

In two minutes they were speeding toward Dripping Springs.

RAZE TOLD BRASH to make himself at home while he threw some stuff into a bag that would fit in his side saddle. "Won't take long. You're welcome to what you can find."

True to his word, Raze was ready to go in six minutes.

"What'd you wanna show me?" Brash asked.

"Walk around here with me," Raze said.

They walked around to the front of the building that had been Farrell's Auto Repair.

Once they were standing in front, Raze said, "There's this place on the other side of Kerrville. It's an ice house called The Lupe."

Brash's eyes slid to Raze. "Yeah?" he said slowly.

"You think a place like this could be a place like that?"

Brash didn't want to spook his friend by being overly excited. So he kept every bit of the joy and optimism he was feeling internally contained. "A place like that? Maybe." Brash walked over to what had been the office door. "Let me in?"

Raze unlocked the door. Brash stepped in and took a look around. It was almost the same identical size and shape of The Lupe. Same number of bay doors. Located on the main drag, which was good. But on the outer edge of the main drag, which was also good.

"Could be fortuitous that Hole in the Wall closed up

six months ago. Hap's wife wanted to live in Colorado. So they went. Kinda left a hole."

"Funny."

"I try. You're thinkin' to use The Lupe as a kind of model?"

"I was."

"So you're thinking food, music, drink, dancin'…"

"Was."

"That's a lot of movin' parts. But it has possibilities. I might be inclined to want to invest."

"I may not need an investor." That was, perhaps, the last thing Brash was expecting to hear. "Uncle Farrell left some cash. I guess he did okay, but liked the simple life."

"Well, what do you know?"

"Think my biggest problem maybe isn't money. It's not knowin' how to get from here to there."

Brash nodded and slapped Raze on the back. "I'll be chewin' on it while we're ridin'. You spend some time with Rescue and Bless. Then I'll take you to lunch and we'll talk some more."

"That…" Raze seemed unsure what to say, but finally decided on, "Thanks."

WHEN BRASH CAME to fetch Raze to go to lunch, he said, "How's it going?"

Raze shook his head. "The dog is a marvel. But that is one seriously messed up dude."

Brash chuckled. "He's part of the test. If people want our dogs bad enough to put up with Rescue, we figure they're going to be good owners."

"Where're you takin' me?"

"Where you want to go?"

"Someplace where we can eat outside."

"Yep. Sounds right."

BRASH LED THE way to a taco stand by the river with picnic tables under the low-hanging trees.

"This one of yours?" Raze asked as he dismounted.

"You won't be disappointed. In fact, I'm bettin' you'll be back after today."

With baskets full of tacos they took a seat by the

river.

"Been thinkin' about your proposition," Brash said.

"Yeah?"

"And I've got some ideas to throw out, but there's somethin' I gotta ask."

Raze looked wary. "Alright."

"You sure you want to get into this?" Raze relaxed visibly when he heard the question wasn't personal. "'Cause it's the kind of life where there's no day off. There's no vacation. There's no time out. Your life is the business and the business is your life. Long ass days full of headaches and problems you never saw comin'."

Raze thought about that for a couple of minutes while he ate. "It's not like there are a lot of demands on my time. Matter of fact, all I got is time."

"Maybe now. But someday there may be a woman…"

"Ain't gonna be no woman."

Brash didn't entirely believe that, but Raze was so adamant about it, he let it go.

"Assuming that's true, let me move on to the next

question. Do you have any experience in the restaurant, bar, or music club business?"

"Not a lick."

"That doesn't worry me as much as the uncertainty of whether or not you'll like it once you're into it."

"Not a child, Brash."

"Not sayin' you are."

"It's what I wanna do."

"You gotta admit this came on kinda fast."

Raze shrugged. "That don't make it untrue."

"And you might not be interested in a woman, but that dog is a kind of family. You can't just leave her alone like a stuffed toy. It's a commitment."

"Brash. Do you understand the meaning of patron-izing?"

"Yes."

"This is startin' to cross into insult territory."

Brash nodded. "Don't take offense. We vet all the people we sell our dogs to. Anyhow, if you're sure about this ice house thing. Really sure. Understandin' that it's a whole other world away from auto repair, then I can get you a team to make it happen."

"A team?"

"Yeah. Small business people like helpin' each other. First off, it just so happens that I'm married to a bar owner."

Raze gaped. "No shit?"

Brash nodded. "They serve food, too. So she can help get you set up. Figure out how to outfit the kitchen and the bar. What you're gonna need to buy and where to buy it. What kind of help you need, what to look for, how to hire. My secretary can help with permits and such. She does that kind of thing all the time."

"You got a secretary," Raze stated as if asking for confirmation.

"Yes. Her name is Beatrice. You'll get to know her before this is over." Brash ran a napkin over his mouth. "The music thing. I don't have a connection there, but you just happen to be sittin' in the best place this side of Nashville if you're lookin' for lots of good hungry talent just dyin' to work even if it's on the cheap."

Raze was nodding. "My thoughts exactly."

"You have any experience bookkeeping?"

"Yeah. I kept books at the shop."

"Good. One less thing to worry about. I was thinkin' we should take a ride over to The Lupe on Saturday night on a scout mission. Everybody who wants to go. Get the lay of the land."

Raze came close to smiling. "Sounds good."

"When I talk to Brigid tonight I'll get her to ballpark how much you're gonna need for kitchen and bar equipment, tables, chairs, plates, and whatnot. You're gonna need a designer, a contractor, and a budget. You're also gonna need a first class sound system. Bands'll play for cheap, but only if they sound good."

"You got people for all that stuff?"

"Matter of fact I do. Got a contractor who'll treat you right. No cut corners. No overcharging. No puttin' you off for other jobs." Brash waved at somebody over at the taco stand and gave them a chin lift. "Unrelated to the subject at hand, you're also gonna need to fence off some of your property for your dog and get a dog door installed so she can come and go. Better put in eight feet because German Shepherds can be climbers. And I'm sure I don't have to tell you that she cannot ride on your bike."

Raze looked a little stricken. "I wouldn't do that."

"Well, of course not. It just had to be said. Got a name for the place?"

"Hadn't thought about it."

Brash grinned. "I got the perfect name. Raze & Ruin Roadhouse. We'll get a designer to do a Triple R brand and use it on everything."

Raze sat back. "Raze & Ruin. You sure?"

"It's a natural."

BRASH FOUND PEOPLE who could put in a fence and a dog door before Raze brought Bless home.

As the project began to take shape Raze and Brash hammered out a partnership. Raze would keep the cash he inherited as working capital to get underway and establish a solid footing. Brash would fund the build out and provide mentorship in exchange for twenty-five percent ownership, but made it clear that it was not a club investment. He was buying in with his own personal money.

Six months later, the SSMC showed up en masse with significant others to support the opening of Raze & Ruin, partying to the sounds of a rockabilly revival band. Thanks to the SSMC putting out word to every recreation ride club in town, the roadhouse was packed.

CHAPTER FOUR

THE LIGHT AT THE END OF THE PARKING LOT

Crowded House – *Don't Dream It's Over*

Present Day

C LOVER LEFT HER phone in the apartment she thought she'd never see again and left her car in the exorbitantly expensive parking garage in Brooklyn, reasoning that criminals might have access to police resources and be able to arrange to have a bulletin issued. Even if she obscured the license plate with mud or forged a paper plate, which any person with third grade computer skills could do, easily, they might look for her make and model.

That had her thinking the choice to buy a 'classic' Jeep Renegade, vintage early seventies, painted school bus yellow, was questionable. Yes. It was cute as could be. It was also, arguably, the most uniquely trackable vehicle in the entire United States.

She couldn't rent a car or use credit cards or the ATM. She knew this because, like any red-blooded American girl, she'd watched TV. And been to the movies. A lot.

No credit or debit or ATM left two options. Cash on hand and Greyhound. Luckily she had some cash. There wasn't a lot left, but there was enough to get far, far away.

Trying to pare a life down to what would fit in a rolling duffel wasn't easy. She made some hard choices. She couldn't say she didn't look back. She stood at the door of her apartment for a long time looking over things she'd never see again. Stuff from fire sales. Stuff left by the curb. Stuff she made herself. She tried to focus on the word that held the pattern together. Stuff.

She told herself the tangibles were meaningless in the big picture that included life and death, took a deep breath of resolve, fought tears back, and walked away pulling her duffel. It was the first time she'd ever contemplated that there might be an upside to not having a family, at least none who cared about her. None who would miss her or report her missing.

Just to be sure her landlord didn't report her missing, she left a note.

Great job opportunity overseas, but I have to leave now. Please re-let the apartment and give away everything not wanted.

It was a hard note to write because everything left *was* wanted. By *her*.

A fresh bout of tears threatened to form, but she fought them back. She reasoned that there would be time to feel sorry for herself later. She bought a prepaid phone and boarded a bus bound for Texas. She didn't know why she'd headed for Texas. It just seemed like the kind of place that would be anathema to the people who might want to look for her.

After a full forty-eight hours of watching alien landscape through a bus window, wallowing in the fact that she was completely alone in the world, she got off a bus in Austin, Texas. A bus ride from New England to Austin is ample opportunity to review options.

Clover's assessment was that she was a person without much of a future before the 'incident'. Now she was a person without a past as well. Exhausted and looking rough as could be, she'd asked herself a thousand times what she was doing and she always came up with the same answer.

Clover was not an adventurer. She'd never been further away from New Jersey than the eastern border of Connecticut. She liked routine and predictability. She liked getting her coffee the same way, at the same time, from the same barista, every morning. She didn't like change and she didn't like uncertainty.

What could motivate such a person to leave everything behind and hop a bus for parts unknown? Only one thing. Fear.

After claiming her bag she found the taxi stand and asked a woman smoking a cigarette on the sidewalk, "Are you from here?"

"Yeah," said the smoker.

"I need a motel kind of close by in a neighborhood that's not too scary."

The smoker grinned. "Not too scary, huh?" Clover nodded. "Turn around."

Clover looked behind her. There was an America's Best Value motel at the other end of the block. Turning back to the woman, she smiled.

"Perfect. Thanks."

"Sure."

The motel manager wanted to see ID. Of course. Clover explained that she'd lost her ID, but that she was paying cash.

"It's policy, ma'am," said the clerk, who was about the same age as Clover.

"I get that. And normally I'm all about policy, but I can't produce an ID that I lost. I could pay a surcharge though. An inconvenience fee?"

She hoped the clerk was bright enough to take her meaning.

Apparently he was. "We might work that out. Fifty dollars cash is our normal surcharge for no ID."

She glared at the guy. Fifty dollars would double the price of the room, but she didn't have a choice and he was primed and ready to take personal advantage of that fact.

"I can't argue with surcharge policy, can I?"

He smiled in a way that resembled gloating. "No, ma'am."

She put a hundred and one dollars on the counter in front of him, two fifties and a one. She knew fifty of that wouldn't make it to the cash drawer, but that was the deal.

After dumping her bag in the second floor room she got for fifty-one bucks, she headed to the IHOP next door. She was sure there was some great local joint close by, but she was hungry, tired, and something tried, true, and familiar seemed to fill the bill.

She grabbed a Greensheet out of the rack stand on the way inside. The greeter looked up, handed her a menu, gave a halfhearted wave toward the back and said, "Anywhere you want."

Sliding into an empty booth next to a window, she

took the side facing away from the room so she wouldn't have to make eye contact. There were men in the world who thought that when a woman traveled alone or ate alone, it was an open invitation for company.

Her gaze was pulled away from the menu when she saw food go by that looked and smelled scrumptious. When the waitress stopped by her table and said, "What can I get you, hon?" Clover said, "What's that they're having?"

The waitress looked back over her shoulder. "Chicken and waffles."

"Is it good?"

With a small shrug the waitress said, "Sure," like she'd never given a thought to whether the food was good or not.

"Okay. I'll have that. And a small salad. First."

"Dressing."

"Ranch. On the side."

"What are you having to drink?"

"Water's okay."

"Back in a few." She hurried away.

True to her word, the waitress was back in a few with Clover's water and salad. By the time she'd finished her salad, the chicken and waffles had arrived.

While she ate she went through the Greensheet classifieds, which was really the point of the publication, for cars for sale. She knew what she was looking for. Something so common nobody would look twice. And cheap. Very cheap.

By the time she'd finished dinner, she was pretty sure she'd picked the one.

A 1993 Toyota Camry XLE silver sedan, with just one hundred eighty-three thousand six hundred and ten miles on it. Fully loaded, whether the bells and whistles worked or not, for just eight hundred dollars. AS IS.

Supposedly it had no accident or damage reported. One owner and regular service. One thing was sure. The price was right.

When she got back to the room she dialed the number in the ad.

"Yeah?" It was a youngish-sounding guy.

"I'm calling about the car?" she said. "The car for sale?"

"Oh. Yeah. I have a car for sale."

"I know. This may be a silly question, but… does it run?"

"Yeah. It'll get you where you wanna go."

"How do you know where I want to go?"

"Well…"

"Never mind. I'm just, um, kidding. Why are you selling?"

"It belonged to my grandmother and she…"

"Stop! Don't say any more. I don't want to hear the rest. I want the car. I'll give you eight hundred in cash."

"You will?"

"Yes. But you'll have to bring it to me."

There was a pause. "Uh, where are you?"

"I'm at the America's Best Value motel in Austin. It's close to I35 and 290."

"You're really gonna buy the car?"

"I really am."

"And you're not gonna dicker?"

"No. I'm not gonna, um, dicker."

"I guess I could bring you the car."

"And the title."

"Yeah. And the title. But you'll have to give me a ride back to my other car."

"And where's that?"

"Dripping Springs."

Dripping Springs. She liked the sound of it. "How far is that?"

"Miles? About twenty-five. Minutes? Depends on the time of day. Could be an hour. Freeways through town are slow goin' these days."

"You got a deal."

"You better be there."

"I will be. What time?"

"I can break away and come up there around eleven."

"That works. Room 213. You've got to be here before twelve or I'll have to pay for another day."

"Yeah. No problem. 213."

"You'll call me if you're going to be late?"

AFTER TWO FULL days on a bus, Clover slept like the dead. She didn't know if she'd always feel safe, but she felt secure for the moment.

At ten thirty the next morning she'd showered, had pancakes at the IHOP, repacked, and was ready to go when her phone rang.

"Hello?"

"Yeah. This is Henry. The guy with the car."

"Uh-huh?"

When Henry discerned that Clover wasn't giving her name, he went on. "Somethin's come up here and I'm not gonna be able to get away until later."

"How much later?"

"Eight."

"Tonight? Eight tonight?"

"Yeah. I'm sorry. Can't be helped, but I feel bad about it. So you can deduct the charge for the motel from the eight hundred."

"It's a hundred and one dollars."

"A night?"

"Yeah."

"Okay. I'll sell you the car for seven twenty-five."

She sighed. That seemed reasonable and Henry did sound sorry. "Okay. Eight o'clock. If they give me a different room, I'll let you know. Otherwise, 213."

The clerk, a woman she hadn't seen, was happy to let her keep room 213. Since Clover was already checked in, the new manager made an assumption that she'd presented ID. So she charged just the daily rate of fifty-one dollars, with a smile.

On the way back to her room, she debated the morality of telling Henry that she'd only been asked for an additional fifty-one dollars. Then she decided that her new policy was to tack on a twenty-five dollar surcharge for inconvenience. She'd use the money for lunch and dinner at the IHOP.

Clover supposed four meals in a row would probably set some sort of IHOP record. *I should get a plaque with my name on it.*

The Texas map she'd bought at the stop in Waco was spread out on the motel room bed so that she could decide where to go after returning Henry to the car he wasn't selling. There were a lot of assumptions in that exercise. She had to begin by assuming that Henry would show up with the car and then go further to assume that the car would make it to Dripping Springs. The words AS IS in capital letters kept flashing across her mind.

Saying that she knew nothing about cars was an understatement. She'd lived most of her life taking public transportation and barely knew how to drive, much less take care of a car. Or know whether it was likely to leave her by the side of the road.

"The price is right," she said to herself out loud every time she had second thoughts. The price was right, the color was right, the age and shape was right. It was the perfect car to go unnoticed.

Since she had several hours and nothing to do, she decided to start out clean and laundered. She knew the motel had a coin washer and dryer because the clerk mentioned it when she extended her stay for another night.

After taking all the clean clothes out of the duffel,

she was left with enough dirty clothes to fill a washer. Most of what she'd decided to take with her was in the hamper. It would be because her favorite things had been worn recently. She wasn't anticipating a crisis that required a "go bag". So she normally let laundry pile up until the weekend.

The clerk on duty in the office, whom she hadn't seen before, exchanged a five dollar bill for some coins. On the way out of the office with her change she grabbed one of every sightseeing brochure in the rack, just so she'd have something to do while she was babysitting laundry.

Once the laundry was started she sat down with her brochures and read every one in detail. The idea of being a tourist was oddly appealing. She'd been to the beach and to amusement parks, but she'd never taken a vacation per se. Most people would ask how it was possible to get an anthropology degree without travel-ing. The bottom line was that she'd been good at school, but never had personal resources or family support to supplement travel. Without that, students on academic scholarships like herself weren't going anywhere except to a second job.

She got hot sitting in the laundry room. There was no air conditioning. Or it wasn't working. Either way, her hair was hanging limp around her face by the time she'd spent forty-five minutes listening to the dryer tumble.

She folded clothes, put them back in her rolling duffel so that it was ready to go and headed back to her room for a shower.

Henry showed at three minutes after eight. She opened the door and looked him up and down while he was looking her up and down.

"You're Henry," she said.

"Yeah. You're my buyer. Right?"

"That's right. You've got the title with you?"

"Uh-huh." He looked over his shoulder. "I'm parked out here. You want to see it?"

"I want to do a lot more than see it."

"Let's go then," he said.

She took a last look around the room as she was

grabbing her purse, just to make sure she wasn't leaving anything, and pulled the duffel out onto the landing.

"I don't suppose you'd like to play gentleman and carry this for me, would you?"

Henry looked at Clover, raised his eyebrows, looked at the duffel, and smiled. "Sure. I'll heft it." He lifted it onto his shoulder easily. "This way."

The car wasn't much to look at, but it was exactly as represented. She'd find out if it worked or not because, according to her calculations, it was a forty-five minute drive from where they were to Dripping Springs.

Henry threw the duffel in the back seat and pulled the title out of the glove compartment. "It's already signed," he said. "Just give me the money and it's yours."

"Not so fast. We have a drive to make. That'll give me a chance to make sure I'm buying a car that works. I'll pay you when we get there."

He huffed and rolled his eyes before saying, "You want to drive. Or me?"

Henry seemed harmless enough, but he was a guy,

and one who was strong enough to lift her duffel like it was nothing. Her intuition wasn't giving her any danger signals, so her caution was more policy than genuine concern. She reasoned that she'd be less vulnerable *not* driving.

"You drive," she said.

"Fine by me."

The car could have used a good detailing, but at least Henry wasn't a smoker. And there weren't used condoms all over the back floorboards. Always a plus.

He interrupted that train of thought by asking, "Where are you headed?"

"Haven't decided yet."

For the next half hour Henry talked about life as he knew it. He was a Dripping Springs native who had no desire to be anywhere else.

"My girlfriend would be mad about me drivin' you back if she saw how cute you are."

Clover didn't know what to say to that. So she said, "Have you done regular oil changes and maintenance?"

"Yeah. I know how to do that stuff."

"Why are you selling?"

"My girlfriend and I are gettin' married. We're gonna share her car and use the money from this car for stuff."

"Oh. Well. Congratulations."

A light rain started to fall. Just enough to need the wipers on as they pulled into a crowded parking lot of a place all lit up with neon and string lights.

Clover leaned down to read the sign through the windshield. "Raze & Ruin."

"Yeah," Henry grinned. "It's a roadhouse. Busy on weekends. Like tonight. Good food. Good drink. Good times."

"Good times," she repeated wistfully in a way that said she didn't expect to ever know good times again.

"Well," Henry prompted, "here we are." He pulled the title out again and turned the overhead light on.

Clover looked it over. It seemed right. *God.* She hoped it was real.

"Okay." She handed over the money. Henry took it and looked at it like he wasn't sure what to do. "Go ahead. It won't hurt my feelings if you count it."

He smiled, looking relieved that he'd gotten permission. "All here. So have a nice trip then. Wherever you're goin'. There's over half a tank of gas. In this car that'll take you pretty far."

"Thanks, Henry."

"I didn't get your name."

She glanced down at the title. The date was the seventh of April.

"Avril," she said.

He smiled. "Nice doin' business with you, Avril. See ya round."

He left the key in the ignition, got out, and disappeared into the night.

Within seconds rain had obscured the view out the windshield giving the world an opaque, abstract look. She got out, ran around, and slid into the driver's seat of her new ride. After moving the seat and back forward, adjusting the mirrors, and putting on her seatbelt, she turned the ignition.

The engine spluttered three times and died.

She sat there, gaping at the wipers, which continued to slap back and forth, operating on battery only.

"You have got to be kidding me," she said. Then shaking her head, "No. No. No. No. I refuse to accept this reality. This cannot be happening to me."

Taking a deep breath she turned the key. For a second she thought it was going to start. Then it spluttered three times and died. She turned the ignition off and withdrew the key. With luck, maybe Henry was still around. Maybe she could catch him and get her money back before he disappeared. Or maybe there was a trick to starting the car that he forgot to mention.

She locked the doors, got out, and ran toward the lights wishing she had one of those cute little umbrellas that collapsed to practically nothing.

CHAPTER FIVE

THE GIRL WITH THE BROKE DOWN CAR

Chris Isaak – *Wicked Game*

I T WAS FRIDAY night at the roadhouse, which meant that it was crowded. But when Clover walked through the door, she immediately caught Raze's eye. She was standing there like a flashing neon sign. She looked lost, but that was not her most notable feature. Her most notable feature was the face of an angel matched with a complete set of unbelievably suckable curves outlined by clothes that were clinging because of being a little damp.

When she looked back over her shoulder, Raze figured that meant that there was a guy outside parking a ride and that he'd be following her in any minute. No guy showed, but she seemed to be looking for somebody.

Raze knew he should have looked away, but he hesitated a second too long and caught her eye. As soon as he did, she came walking his way.

"Hey," she said. "Do you know a guy named Henry?"

"Got a last name?" Raze managed to ask without implying friendliness on any level.

"Yes. It's, um…" She struggled to remember the name on the title. "Boyd. I think it's Boyd."

"You *think* it's Boyd?"

"Look. I just bought a car from the guy. Now it's sitting in the parking lot and it won't start."

Raze was having this conversation while he was continuing to pull beers because Marjorie had called in with some lame excuse, which meant she was fired. For the fourteenth time. Employees couldn't bail on weekends.

"You got any experience slingin' drinks?"

"What?" She looked confused.

"I'm short of help. I can't look at your car tonight.

We're busy. Since you're not going anywhere, how about grabbing an apron and helping out? Standard pay."

"No. I don't have any experience, um, slinging drinks. I'm not even sure what that is."

Raze gave up a disgusted sigh. "You good with people?"

To that question she gave a cute little smirk. Raze figured that cute little smirk was a powerful survival characteristic that had served her well. He shook his head, thinking he'd be sorry but knowing he had no choice, and handed her an apron.

She took it, looked at it like she didn't know what to do with it. After a second or two she raised those big blue eyes to his and said, "I don't have a place to stay."

Christ. She *was* lost.

He looked away so she wouldn't think she had him by the balls and let go with a stream of cuss words – all in his head.

"Do a good job and you can sleep in the studio in the back. For *tonight*," he said. "Tomorrow morning I'll take a look at your car."

She gave Raze a hug like she was grabbing onto a lifesaver, and filled his nose with her rainy green apple feminine shampoo smell. He did a good job of hiding it, but that hug knocked him to his ass. She was just some woman coming off the road. He knew this. But there was something...

He pushed her away. Gently. "Just for *tonight*."

Raze's voice was gruff and sounded harsh. *Good.* She didn't need to get the idea that his roadhouse was some plushy crash pad.

She managed to get the apron on and looked down at her purse.

"Here. Give me that," Raze said. "I'll keep it here behind the bar. Don't worry. It'll be safe." He gave her a tray of empty mugs and a pitcher of beer. "Take this to that table over there."

"The one in the corner?"

"No. The one with the guy in the red baseball cap." She turned to go. "And don't let anybody feel you up or pat your butt."

She turned back, blue eyes having flown wide. "What?"

Raze wondered if he was looking at Alice down the rabbit hole. She was lost *and* innocent. Of all the roadhouses in the world, how did she manage to walk into his?

"What's your name?" Raze said.

She glanced over his shoulder at the bottles lined up on mirrored shelves. "Gin," she said.

Assuming it was short for Virginia, he said, "Okay. Hustle back here fast as you can."

Things were happening too fast for her to question. If it wasn't a twist, it was a turn. She didn't have a car that ran or the money to buy another. But she did have a place for the night and, if the heavenly smell of onion rings was any indication, at some point she might get fed.

Two hours later requests for food had died down.

Raze motioned her over. "You had dinner?"

"Maybe. But it was a *long* time ago."

"Take a break. Go get somethin' in the back before

they start bringin' down the kitchen."

She nodded and did exactly that. She introduced herself to a kid named Julio and a relic named James.

"What do ya want?" James asked.

She looked around. "What do you have?"

"Darlin'. You've been cartin' food all night. You know what we have."

"I guess I mean, what's easy?"

James looked at Julio, who grinned and shrugged. Then he said, "Gotta love an indecisive woman."

"Wait a minute! Who are you calling indecisive? I'll have a cheeseburger medium well. More well than medium. Yellow mustard. Lettuce. Tomato. No onion. Oh, and hickory sauce. Somebody ordered that and it smelled really good. And I'd really like some of those onion rings I've been 'carting' around all night."

"You want onion rings instead of fries, but you don't want onion on your burger," James observed in a monotone.

"It's not the same thing."

"Whatever you say."

"Is this like hazing?" Her gazed flicked to Julio.

"No. It ain't like hazin'," Julio said. "He's just a cranky old shit who gives everybody a hard time. What do you want to drink? We got soft drinks and root beer in a wood barrel on ice. Over there by the bar. Lemonade. And some orange crush."

"Yeah. I know," she said, plopping down. "I just don't want it bad enough to go get it."

Julio chuckled. "Tenderfoot. You'll get used to the routine."

"No. I won't," she said. "This was a one night stand."

"Okay."

"Really."

"Okay."

"I mean it."

"How much did you make in tips tonight?"

"I don't know."

"Why don't you look?"

She looked down at the deep pocket in her apron and stuck her hand in. What she found there was shocking. She supposed she'd been so panicked about trying to keep up with a job she didn't know how to do and avoid grabby hands, that she'd just stuffed money in the pocket without stopping to think about it.

After she straightened out wadded-up bills, sorted, and counted, there was over two hundred dollars there. She looked up at Julio.

"Yes, ma'am," he said. "Weekend nights are good. Our customers are generous with tips if you halfway try. And Raze don't make you share like a lot of places do. You get to keep it. All of it."

"Damn," she said.

"Still in a big hurry to get gone?" Julio asked as he set her burger and onion rings in front of her.

After counting three times, she folded the money up and stuck it into her jeans pocket, thinking that she could hide out in Dripping Springs just as easily as someplace else.

"I don't know," she said honestly. "What about the frowny guy?"

"Frowny guy?" Julio's brow opened up when he realized who she meant. "That's Raze." He laughed. "The owner. James," he turned to the relic who was busy wire brushing the gas grill, "she called Raze frowny guy."

James just grunted and continued working without looking up.

"Either this is the best burger I've ever had in my life," she said while chewing, "or I'm so hungry I'm no longer a good judge."

"Yeah. James keeps 'em comin' back. That's why he gets the big bucks. Right, James?"

James grunted. And didn't look up.

"Hey. Do you know a guy named Henry Boyd?"

Before Julio could answer the double hinge door swung open. "You done yet?" Raze said. "Got customers waitin'."

"Wow," she said sarcastically, "I can't imagine why you were short on help tonight."

Julio snorted. James stopped what he was doing and looked up. Raze's features went slack. He was still trying to decide what to say and how to say it when she ducked under his arm on the way back to work.

At one o'clock the band quit playing and started breaking down. Raze turned on the jukebox. He always said there was nothing worse for roadhouse business than quiet. When there was no band, there was jukebox. When there was a band, the jukebox came on when they took breaks.

She was so grateful that she'd happened to put on tennis shoes and jeans. Even so, she was falling down tired by the time the door was locked and everybody was gone except for herself and frowny guy.

"You got some stuff with you? Stuff you need to get for the night?"

"Um, yes."

"Come on. I'll walk you out there." Raze reached under the bar, retrieved the purse that was stowed there earlier, and handed it to her.

In silence they walked to the lone car left in the parking lot. When they reached it, he said, "Give me your key."

She fished the key out of her purse and handed it over. He had to adjust the seat for long legs before he could slide behind the wheel, but when he did, one twist of the key in the ignition and the car purred to life like a million dollar Formula One racer.

"Seems okay to me," Raze said.

She had no explanation. "I don't know how… Well, thanks then. I guess I'll be on my way."

"You will not be on your way."

"Yes." She nodded. "I will."

"Where you gonna go at two thirty in the damn mornin'? It's not the Vegas strip. It's Dripping Springs."

He had a point.

"Well…"

"Get in. I'll drive you around to the studio. You can get a good night's sleep. When you wake up tomorrow, if you want to be on your way, nice knowin' ya. If you want a job, we'll talk."

"Okay."

She got in on the passenger side and one minute later they were stopped at the door of the studio.

"I live in that house right over there." He pointed. He wasn't sure why he was telling her that. It just seemed like the thing to say at the time.

He unlocked the studio, switched on the lights, set her duffel down, and waited while she looked around.

It was neat. Functional. Even nice, if a bit… teenagerish? Like an adolescent had once lived there. She spotted a photograph of a high school football team and concluded that she was looking at frowny guy's history.

She bent over and squinted to try and pick him out of the photo and, yes, there he was in the center of the back row, probably because of his tall frame, handsome boyish features free of frown. He was standing next to a heartthrob who was about the same height, who looked to be the essence of bad boy walking. And he was smiling.

So you didn't always wear a permafrown. Wonder what happened to you, frowny guy.

"IT's CLEAN," HE said, watching her, trying to see the studio through her eyes and wondering what she was thinking.

She nodded. "Thank you. This is, um, nice of you."

Raze didn't want her thinking that he was a soft touch. "Nothin' nice about it. I needed help tonight. You showed up. Providence. So, if you're good, I'll be goin'." When she didn't respond, he pressed further. "You good?"

"Yes. It's just that. That doesn't look like much of a lock."

He turned toward the studio door. She was right. It wasn't much of a lock. He'd never had cause to give that any thought. His frown deepened.

"You worried?"

"I… Maybe."

"Okay." He picked up her duffel. "Come on."

"Wait. Where are we going?"

"My house. You can sleep there. I'll sleep here tonight. And trust me, my house is the safest place you'll ever sleep."

"It is? I mean, no. I don't want to put you out of your own house." She was trying to slow things down, but learning that Raze was a force of nature who made decisions fast, acted fast, and nothing stood in his way.

She was rushing to keep up with him as he headed toward his house. Since he was carrying everything she owned in the world, she had no choice but to follow the duffel.

"You're not. This is my house, too." He stopped abruptly at his door and put the duffel down. When he lowered his voice and said, "Come here," she felt an unwelcome but pleasant shudder travel through her body.

"Why?"

"'Cause you're about to meet the reason why this is the safest place for miles around."

He unlocked his door, cracked it open and said, "Got company, Bless."

He opened the door further and stepped in to greet a gorgeous, if huge, German Shepherd, who was ecstatic to see frowny guy, but also curious enough about the woman to keep her focus trained on the guest.

"This is my dog."

"I see that."

"She's special."

"And really, really, really big."

"She won't hurt you. At least not now that I've introduced you."

"That's comforting."

"She's extremely protective," Raze said. She followed him to the bedroom since that was where her duffel was going. "Part instinct. Part training. You can sleep sound. Once I leave and close this door, nobody's comin' in here tonight besides me." That didn't come out the way he intended. So to clarify, he added, "And I won't be back until morning. Slept on the sheets once, but I'd had a shower. So. They're fresh enough. Hope that's okay."

Raze knew the place was clean and orderly. He knew the difference between clean, orderly, and not thanks to time in the service. He had a service that came once a week to deep clean, but he kept the place presentable.

"I don't really feel right about this."

"Look. Long night. We're tired. Too tired to argue. Go to bed. I'm doin' the same." And with that he walked out and left Clover alone with Bless.

The dog looked at her with expectation. Waiting to see what she'd do next?

"I guess I'm going to bed now. If that's okay?" she said to the dog. Bless climbed onto the loveseat that sat against the wall. "Is that where you sleep?" Bless put her head down on her paws. "I take that as a yes." She glanced toward what appeared to be a half bath, shower only, attached to the bedroom. "I'm just going to get my stuff and brush my teeth."

She opened her duffel, but decided she was too tired to brush teeth. She was too tired to change clothes as well. So she took off her shoes and her jeans and decided to sleep the way she was.

The second her head hit the pillow she was overwhelmed by frowny guy's scent. Fortunately it was a nice mix of Old Spice and clean masculine musk.

She turned on her side facing the dog and thought that a more prudent person would be terrified of going to sleep a couple of yards away from a giant wolf dog who could tear her throat out with one lunge. How did she know the dog wasn't hormonal? Did dogs suffer from PMS? Or jealousy?

As if Bless could read her mind, she climbed off the loveseat, padded over, put her chin on the bed, and wagged her tail. Clover reached out and ran her hand over the silky head. "Wow. Your hair is amazing. Like the perfect PH balance. What do you use?"

Bless turned and climbed back onto her bed then watched as Clover fell into an exhausted sleep.

CHAPTER SIX

THE GHOST IN THE MACHINE

The Cars – *Drive*

T HE NEXT TIME Clover opened her eyes, there was no dog on the loveseat, light streaming in between blinds, and the smell of coffee brewing. Since the bedroom door had been left open, she could hear the occasional sound of a deep voice talking quietly. She rolled over the other direction and looked at the bedside clock. Eleven forty-five.

She'd slept like the dead. But amazingly, felt good. She considered that, maybe the exercise of running tables at a roadhouse had been good for her after days of sedentary travel. After closing the bedroom door and gathering things from her duffel, she took a too-hot shower that relaxed sore muscles in the most delicious way, moisturized her body head to toe, and pulled her damp hair back into a braid at the nape of her neck.

After packing up all her things and carefully making the bed, she emerged looking fresh and girl-next-door au naturel, dragging her duffel behind her.

Raze was sitting at the dinette. He hoped that stray girl didn't notice his eyes widen when she stepped into the kitchen looking supremely edible. Unconsciously he'd taken to thinking of her as 'stray girl' because it was so much less personal than calling her by name. He couldn't possibly form an attachment to someone he thought of as stray. Even if she was more delicious than a display of handcrafted gelato garnished with fresh fruit under a glass display.

He wasn't sure how he felt about the fact that she looked even better in the light of day. If that was possible. No makeup. No pretense. No explanation as to why a woman like her was buying a beater in a town like Dripping Springs. Traveling alone and tight lipped about it. For a woman. Most women he knew would have already attempted to narrate their entire biographies peppered with details of all their personal business that he really did *not* want to know.

He sat quietly while Bless went over to greet Clover wagging her tail. Clover smiled, "Good morning, you," and gave the dog an affectionate rub down her back. She then turned her attention to Raze. "Good morning."

"Mornin'," he said. "Got coffee. Got breakfast burritos from Grenados." He shoved a white paper bag in her direction.

"Thank you." She looked toward the door. "I really should be going. This has been incredibly generous of you. And I slept really good." She smiled. "Made some money last night. Which will be helpful."

He kicked the chair out. "Sit. You have to have breakfast."

She hesitated, looking from Raze to the chair to the coffee pot to the white paper sack. Everything looked good. Including frowny guy. In spite of the frown.

"Well, I…"

"Don't have cream, but I do have sugar." He watched her eyes go to the coffee pot again. He got up, pulled a mug out of the cabinet and poured a cup, deciding not to take no for an answer. "You want sugar?"

She bit her bottom lip for half a second in indecision before saying, "Yes. Please."

He set the steaming cup and a box of sugar cubes on the table. She smiled. "What?"

"Oh. Sugar cubes. I haven't seen any since I was a kid. My mom got them for tea parties."

Raze grunted at that. "Where was that?"

"Upstate New York."

He turned his head to look at her more closely. "You're a *long* way from home."

"Yes," she acknowledged quietly, without encouraging follow-up questions. "I like your dog."

He glanced over at Bless. "She was a gift from a friend. Well, with some strings attached. She's a breeder. Once a year we have puppies around here."

Clover grinned in a way that let Raze know she approved of puppies. "Puppies! Wow. How many?"

"I understand it varies. This past winter we had six."

98

"Six," she repeated. Then sighed as if to say she would have liked to have seen that and took a sip of coffee.

He shoved the white paper sack in her direction. "How'd you do last night?"

"Well," she opened the top and looked inside. Whatever was wrapped up in paper smelled inviting. As she reached for it, she said, "It was pretty confusing at first. Trying to figure out the code of tables. What to take where. I'm more about the Manhattans than the draft beer, but after about four hours it started to make sense. My feet hurt." She smiled and took a nibble of burrito. "Hmmm. Good."

"Yeah. I really meant, did you make bank?"

Confusion cleared after a few blinks. "Oh. Tips! I had no idea people who wait tables make so much."

"They don't. Well, not usually. For a lot of reasons. And, o'course, weekend nights are busy. Busy means more hustle. More tips." He watched her reactions as he talked. She was definitely not the kind of girl you'd expect to be in her situation. "Don't guess you want to tell me your story."

He saw her entire body tense at the same time the little smile disappeared from her face. "My story?" She was already looking at the door and setting the burrito down.

"You don't have to…"

Standing up, she said, "Thank you so much for…" she looked around, "everything. The bed. The shower. The burrito." She took hold of the handle of her rolling duffel. "The tips." She laughed nervously. "But it's already afternoon and I need to, um, hit the road?"

"Hold on there, stray girl. I didn't mean to scare you."

"You didn't."

"A half-eaten burrito and halfway to the door says otherwise."

"No. Really. I just, um, you know."

"No. I don't know. But that's okay. I don't have to know what's not my business." She looked unsure. "At least finish this burrito. I don't give Bless leftovers and I've already had mine. Some pig gave his life for your breakfast."

She smiled. "If I'm not in your way…"

"You are *not* in my way." He grimaced, realizing that he sounded almost eager for her to stay. And Raze Rouen was not a man who was eager for women to want to stay. Not at all. Still, he had to admit that he was glad when she turned loose of the duffel handle and sat back down. Probably because his uncle had raised him to be polite.

She smiled hesitantly when she picked up the discarded burrito.

"Last night you did okay for somebody with no experience and not lookin' for a job."

There were too many qualifications attached to that comment for it to be called an actual compliment, but she said, "Thanks," bringing her free hand up to cover her mouth so that he wasn't looking at carnitas and scrambled eggs in the first stage of digestion.

"I need help. If you need a job, it's yours." She looked uncomfortable again. "You can't have my house, but you could use the studio. For a while." He sat back, the table hiding the fact that his knee juddered up and down nervously. "I could get a better lock for the door. Maybe put in a security system."

Bless turned and left through the dog door, almost like she was embarrassed for him.

"That's incredibly generous of you, but I don't think I'm, um, what you need." Realizing how that sounded, she amended. "At the roadhouse, I mean." She took a drink of room temperature coffee. "Why'd you call it Raze and Ruin?"

"Friend suggested it. My last name is Rouen." He spelled it out. "I think my great-greats gave up on the French pronunciation. Everyone says 'Ruin'."

"Oh." Her gaze locked with his. "It's your name!"

"Yeah."

"Your parents named you Raze?"

"Not exactly. It's the name that stuck after I started raisin' hell."

"Oh." She looked around for the trash to throw away the wrapper and, not seeing it, put it inside the white paper bag. "Well, then. Gotta go."

He stood quickly and nodded. "If you change your mind, I can always use a rookie server."

"You've been more than nice. Really. Thank you. And I like your dog."

"Yeah." He looked down at the duffel. "I'll get that."

Before she could protest, he'd picked it up and started toward the door.

When she was behind the wheel, he said, "Where are you headed?" The second he said it, he realized he'd violated his promise to avoid personal questions. "Never mind. Wherever it is, safe trip."

"Thanks, again," she smiled and turned the key.

Nothing.

Not even a plaintive grinding.

She leaned forward and put her forehead on the steering wheel.

Raze opened the door. "Want me to try?"

She nodded and got out.

After adjusting the seat, he slid behind the wheel, turned the key, and the car started without protest. "Huh," he said. "Starts for me. Wonder what you're doing wrong."

That caused her blood to shoot straight to boiling range. "I'm not doing anything wrong. How many ways are there to start a car?"

"Well," he said, "apparently there's more than one."

She clenched her teeth and pressed her lips together. "It's probably air in the line."

He looked at her sideways and almost laughed. "What line would that be?"

"I don't know. Maybe you have a better explanation."

"You want to try again?"

"Of course I want to try again. It's *my* car!"

Twice more they played out the folly. The car started for Raze. Refused to make a sound for Clover.

"I guess it's a sign," he said.

"A sign of what?"

"That you're where you ought to be for now."

"You believe in signs," she said drily.

"Not generally, but this is a bona fide mystery."

She cocked her head. "You know Henry Boyd?"

"I might. Why?"

"He's the *gentleman* who sold me this piece of shit. I want my money back."

"Thing is, I'm guessin' that even if we track him down and get him over here, car's gonna start for him and not for you."

"That's what you're guessing?"

"Yeah."

"Well, it's not like you're an expert on car mechanics, is it!" He almost laughed, but somehow managed to keep a straight face. She leaned against the car. "I can't drive a car that won't start." Then she added, "For *me*."

"That's a fact."

She wondered if Raze was going out of his way to be deliberately aggravating or if she was just flustered by the series of events. She hung her head.

I will not cry. I will not cry. I will not cry.

"Look. I know some people who are 'experts at car mechanics'. I'll have them come get it and take it back to the shop for a look."

"I don't have money for expensive car repairs."

"First, you don't know it's gonna be expensive. Second, you could work at the roadhouse tonight. Put some more cushion together. I guess I could let you stay at my place for another night."

"Why would you do that? I mean, I'm not trying to be ungrateful, but that's really generous."

"Just so happens we can be of use to each other. I need help. And you're in a fix."

"Indentured servitude."

"Look…"

"Strike that. I don't know what I'm saying. I'm just, um…"

"Out of sorts."

"Right."

He opened the back door of the Toyota and pulled the duffel out. "Come back in. I'll give my friends a call."

"WHY AREN'T YOU fixin' it yourself?" Press asked.

Raze held the phone closer to his ear and glanced up at his guest. "No tools."

"Uh-huh. You know what you're describin' makes no sense."

"Do know that. And yet I saw it for myself. I'll drive it over there and you can keep it for, you know, a few days."

"A few days? What are you talkin' about? I could build a new car in a few days."

"No more than a few days. The car's owner can't hang around here forever. She has places to go."

After a moment of silence, Press said, "*She* does, does *she*? Okay. I get it. You want me to spend a few days lookin' for a ghost in the machine that causes the car to refuse to turn over, but only when she's behind the wheel."

"Yeah. That's right. 'Cause, like she said, I don't know anything about auto mechanics."

Press chuckled. "I hope you know what the hell you're doin'. Bring it on over."

"Be there shortly." He hung up and looked at Clover. "You can drive my truck. Bless'll ride with you."

"Wait. I can't… A few days?"

"Somethin' pressin?"

She looked down. "Um, no. I just…" He saw her shoulders slump in defeat and had mixed feelings. On the one hand, he didn't like to see her disappointed. On the other hand, he needed somebody who could carry trays and smile at customers. That, he told himself, was his only interest in the matter.

Clover and Bless followed Raze to the SSMC compound. Though only forty-five minutes had passed since the phone call, Press had managed to spread gossip throughout the club so that nine members, including Brant and Brash, happened to be hanging out in the maintenance hangar when they arrived. They were made devilishly giddy by the glares he shot them, each and every one.

She was taken aback by all the men who appeared to be possibly dangerous and underemployed.

"You're not going to introduce us to the lady?" Brash teased Raze.

"She's not interested in gettin' to know you, Brash," he growled in reply.

Brash shrugged, but the broad smile on his face stayed in place. He was enjoying himself way too much. Raze gave him a long look that promised epic retribution at the earliest opportunity.

"Just so I understand the problem," Press said. "Could you show me what happens when you try to start the car? Miss?" He nodded at Clover.

Press had been smirking because he was positive that Raze was making the whole thing up. He cocked his head as she was getting out.

She got in and turned the key.

Nothing.

Press leaned into the open window, face an inch from Clover's and said, "Try it again."

Raze felt a tiny twinge of resentment about that liberty, but reassured himself that he had no reason to care if Press got close to the stray. She was just a random woman he needed to fill in for Marjorie.

"Here. Let me try." He slid in and the car started without hesitation. "Huh." The club members gave each other looks. He nodded at Raze. "Okay. Let me keep it for a few days. I'll give you a call."

Raze gave the slightest chin dip in return and shot everybody a lethal look in parting, but their smirks had turned to puzzled looks laced with a renewed respect.

"Christ," Brant said under his breath to Brash. "What if there really is a ghost in the machine?"

Brash looked at the car and decided he needed to get back to the other things he had on his plate for the day. "Maybe what we need is a priest. Not a grease monkey."

Brant laughed and walked off.

Brash watched Raze and Clover get in the pickup. Bless was in the seat behind the cab with her head out the open window. "You takin' care of my dog?" he shouted.

"Fuck you," Raze said as he climbed in and closed the door.

Brash laughed as he threw a leg over his bike and called the thunder.

BOTH BACK WINDOWS were down, but Bless seemed to

prefer to hang her head out the window on the passenger side. That meant Clover had a perfect view of the dog's windy joy in the side mirror and found herself thinking that Bless had it good. She never had to worry about a single thing in life except doing her job, which was to love and protect frowny guy.

They drove in silence for a while. No radio. Just wind noise from having the back windows down. Raze was first to speak.

"It is strange."

She turned and stared at his chiseled profile and admired the masculine planes a few seconds too long. There was something uncomfortably intimate about being in a vehicle with a man who was a stranger. Even if she had slept in his bed the night before.

"That the car won't start for me?" She turned to face the road ahead. "Yes. I'd say so."

"I'm not a believer in supernatural shit. But... I'm just sayin' it's strange."

"I thought you were saying it's a sign that I'm supposed to wait tables at the roadhouse."

His lips moved just enough to qualify as a smile. "You buyin' that?"

She sighed. "I might not have a choice." After letting that hang in the air for a minute, she said, "I don't want you to think I'm being ungrateful. I mean, I'm glad to have an option that includes food and shelter."

"You hungry?" he said.

"No. We just had breakfast burritos."

"That was an hour and a half ago."

She laughed. "I know. But I'm not a hobbit." He squinted like he didn't understand the reference. "*Lord of the Rings*?"

"Oh. Uh-huh."

"Hobbits eat a lot and eat often."

"So you like kids' movies?"

Clover gaped. "*Lord of the Rings* is not a kids' movie."

"If you say so."

"First, it was a trilogy of very well-written books based on Germanic sagas before it became an incredibly well-crafted trilogy of movies. For everybody. Not just kids."

He looked over at Clover. What he said was, "This important to you?" What he was thinking was that something wasn't adding up. The woman didn't talk like a road stray who'd buy a broke down beater in a borderline rural town like Dripping Springs.

Her answer to the question was a huff.

He had a list of questions he was itching to rapid fire at her and knew she'd close off if he did. Maybe even leave without her car. He wasn't getting any direct answers, but he was collecting puzzle pieces.

He pulled into McAlister's Market and parked.

"What are we doing?" she asked.

He looked over at her as he undid his seatbelt. "They have these places where people get food…"

She rolled her eyes. "If you're going to be a smart guy boss, don't be surprised if you find you have a smart mouth server."

"Okay." He shrugged as if to say that would not be a problem for him.

"So you're getting groceries." He just gave her a

look. "I'll stay with the car?"

"Truck. And no. You will not stay with the truck. How am I gonna know what you want for the house if you stay in the truck?"

"You're going to get what I want for the house?"

"Thought I would."

She grinned. "I'm coming."

"Thought you might. We need to make it snappy. Saturday's always busy, but we got a popular band comin' in tonight."

"So you basically work all the time."

"I'd rather work a lot for myself than work a little bit for somebody else."

She didn't say so, but thought that rang true, regardless of the folksy delivery. Raze had a certain Texas kind of charm that made her lower her guard because she felt very, very far away from New Jersey.

She jumped down from the truck, closed the heavy door, and rushed to keep up with his long strides.

He didn't slow or look to see if she was keeping up, but he did say, "What do you like?"

"Um, Cheetos?"

He came to an abrupt, dead stop before turning to look at her. "No. I meant what do you like to *eat*! Cheetos are not food. It's cardboard with orange chemicals sprayed on top."

Clover started giggling in spite of herself because she wasn't sure Raze was wrong about that. After giving her a look that said he doubted her sanity, he resumed his march toward the entrance.

"Howdy, Raze," said an old guy in passing.

Raze didn't change expression or pace or even turn his head. "Howdy, Mr. Baird."

Inside Raze grabbed a grocery cart. "You like bananas?"

Without waiting for an answer, he put a bunch of bananas in the cart. The rest of the shopping went pretty much like that. He gathered up bacon, eggs, cheese, milk, syrup, and orange juice.

"I like cranberry juice," she said. "And it's good for urinary tract health."

"Too much information," he said, but he pulled a

quart of cranberry juice off the shelf.

When they came to pancakes, he reached for whole wheat, but his hand stopped when she made a grunting sound. "Somethin' wrong with whole wheat?"

"No." She pointed to the blueberry pancake mix. "I just love blueberry."

"But the whole wheat is better for you."

"I'll take vitamins?" she offered.

He didn't think much of that as a compensatory measure, but conceded because he figured that, whatever the reason stray girl didn't want to talk about herself, or even give her last name, she probably deserved a few empty calories and comfort carbs. And she probably wasn't going to keel over before he hired a permanent replacement for Marjorie. So why not?

"Here you go." He handed her the box and she smiled like it was a diamond bracelet. "Don't ever say I never did anything for you."

Her face grew instantly serious and she said, "I wouldn't. You have."

BLESS STUCK HER head through the window for a pet of acknowledgement from Clover. She seemed to be fine with the prospect of adding a female to the pack.

"You can stay here in the house until I get the lock changed on the studio. Tonight'll be even busier. I'm gonna take this dog for a run. Then we'll head over and get you situated on details you might've missed last night, while I'm waiting for deliveries."

"Okay." She nodded.

"Need you to be on shift at six."

"Okay."

WHEN RAZE LEFT to go for a run with Bless, Clover spread her map out on the bed. She had a plan.

Get the car fixed.

Work long enough to save up a thousand dollars in cash.

Then move on.

She'd been studying the map, thinking that her best chance was in the most remote place possible. Some-place that would be anathema to New Jersey. She planned to keep driving west to where populations thinned out to nothing. Maybe close to the New Mexico border. Maybe on the other side.

She supposed her new table waiting skills could come in handy because there might not be a lot of jobs for anthropology majors. Or people with experience answering phones for magazines. She remembered what Julio had said about the fact that it was unusual for a server to earn the tips she got at the roadhouse and decided to factor that in to the plan.

For some reason the view of Raze's stern profile came to mind. She was itching to ask what had happened to make him so frowny. Maybe, if the right time presented itself, she would ask. Maybe she'd decide that Dripping Springs was remote enough.

CHAPTER SEVEN

THE DANCE OF BAYOU BANDITS

Zydeco dancing to Preston Frank Grassroots 2010

I T WAS A clear Goldie Locks kind of night. Not too hot. Not too cool. Just right for opening up the bay doors, which was a good thing because it seemed like half the county showed up to be entertained by the Bayou Bandits and Clover understood why. They were marvelously talented musicians who understood that Saturday nights at the roadhouse are supposed to be about fun and forgetting the troubles that stacked up during the week. And they brought the fun.

By the time Clover had heard people shout, "Gin!" a couple hundred times she was getting used to the idea of that being her name. She decided it might be smart to start thinking of herself that way. Raze had made her a paper label name tag with "Gin" in big blue marker.

She was raking in tips like the world was ending, more than the night before. The customers liked her smile and the fact that she was likeable without having to try too hard.

The roadhouse was running the full complement of staff. There were four servers hustling the tables, two guys tending bar, and a really sweet, bald guy called Dunk who looked the part of beefy bouncer, but probably wouldn't hurt a fly. Besides herself there were two servers who worked part time Friday and Saturday nights, and Marjorie, who'd decided to show up after all, miffed that Raze had given the best tables to the new girl.

The bartenders both looked more "Sixth Street" than Dripping Springs. Both were cute and knew how to make that work for them. The way they flirted with Clover validated her attractiveness and bolstered her self-assurance. She realized she'd been missing that when answering phones at the magazine, going home tired, and making love to a spoon and a carton of ice cream.

She was grateful to be working the inside tables. Fewer steps equaled faster service equaled more turnover equaled more tips. She was a fast learner. She put it together that Marjorie was working the outside tables as punishment for leaving Raze in a bind the night before.

The atmosphere was so charged with life, she almost forgot that she wasn't used to working on her feet for eight hours at a time. But when she stopped for a dinner break, she got the tossed salad with chunks of white meat fried chicken in it. She felt pretty confident she was working off the yummy breading.

For the second night in a row she was just finishing dinner when Raze stuck his head in the kitchen and said something to the effect of, "Not payin' you to shoot the shit with James and Julio."

She looked over her shoulder and said, "Keep your pants on." That caused Julio to snort and James to turn around to see what the boss was going to do.

Raze lifted both eyebrows.

Clover rolled her eyes and grinned at Julio. "Thanks

for dinner, James." He lifted a spatula, but didn't look up.

She wasn't surprised that Raze was aware she'd taken a dinner break. All night long, whenever she'd looked toward the bar, he'd had his eyes locked on her. Like she was his business. His only business.

At first she thought he was staring at her in a supervisory capacity, making sure she didn't mess up too badly. But after a time, she thought she might have seen something else in his eyes. Something more flattering maybe.

Around ten o'clock the Bandits decided to liven things up with a little zydeco. Clover was sliding her tray onto the end of the bar for refill just as Raze had been coming around the end to see how things were going at the register.

Nothing could have surprised her more than being grabbed by Raze and being pulled straight into zydeco dance. Within three steps they were on the dance floor with her protesting.

"Wait!" she said. "I don't, um, know how to dance

to this music."

"It's easy, stray girl," Raze said. "Just do this."

He never stopped, just continued dancing, carrying her along until she began to match his steps, feeling the syncopated rhythm. Before a full minute had passed, she'd picked up the basic steps. The initial panic had melted into a happy anxiety, noticing that pretty much everybody in the place had stopped to watch.

No one had seen Raze dance before. Had no idea he could, which was why the entire establishment had come to a standstill and cleared the floor.

Clover didn't know if the customers were laughing because they were having a good time or if they were laughing at her initial awkwardness. She knew they weren't laughing at Raze. First, because he was nothing less than scrumptious in his jeans, ropers, and midnight blue Henley with sleeves pushed up his muscled fore-arms. The knit shirt clung to the hard planes of his body that, she supposed, he kept fit running the dog around. And, second, because he knew how to dance zydeco and look good doing it, which came down to being masculine, rhythmic and in charge. She'd learned in the twenty-four hours since she'd met Raze that he didn't have any issues with the "in charge" part.

He'd picked up Cajun dancing almost by accident when his Guard unit had gone to New Orleans years before for a training week that involved flood response preparedness. A woman in the unit, originally from Louisiana, had insisted he give it a try. Raze hadn't danced since and honestly didn't know what came over him, but there he was on the dance floor enjoying the fact that his employees and customers were having a good time.

Feeling that stray girl was comfortable enough with the moves, he twirled her around twice without breaking step. The joy of the carefree moment, the pleasure of the crowd, and the laughter of the beautiful girl in his hands must have overcome him because he answered her laughter with a grin.

What Clover saw was no ordinary smile. It was an expression that halted time and magnetized angels. It seemed that frowny guy had been holding out on looks that were unmatched in her catalog of noticeable boy memories, hiding out behind a frown. It wasn't just the transformation of his face into heart-stopping beauty brought on by a flash of white teeth and light in his eyes. His lopsided grin also conveyed a sexy cockiness that was her undoing.

Somehow she managed to finish the dance without making a fool of herself. When it was over, the entire roadhouse clapped, hooted, stomped and shouted.

Raze danced her right back to the tray she'd left on the bar, twirled her one last time, said, "Thank you for the dance," and disappeared into the back leaving her confused, breathless, and the center of attention, which caused a full body blush.

"So," said Luke, the bartender, winking one heart-throb turquoise eye, "boss's got a thing for you, huh?"

"Uh, no, uh."

"Can't blame him," Luke said as he was topping off a draft. "Wish I'd spoken for you first."

She knew he was teasing and it was empty words, but she ducked her head feeling a sudden shyness coming over her. "It was just a dance."

Luke barked out a laugh. "Darlin', if that's what you think, then you *really* don't know Raze Rouen. That was not *just* a dance." He jerked the draft handle. "It was a damn miracle."

The other bartender, Carl, laughed at that.

Hearing one of her orders called up, she gave a little smile and turned to load her tray and get back to work. It was impossible to forget about the dance when for the rest of the night, people were remarking on how fun it was to see Raze dance. She nodded and smiled, but it weighed on her heart that people in the community cared about Raze and loved seeing the frown gone from his face, even for a short time.

The other servers teased her about wishing they were in line for a dance, but in the case of at least one, she thought the teasing was thinly veiled jealousy.

She figured out early how to handle grabby hands. Dump a mug of beer in their lap and say, "Oops." The first time she did it, the guy stood up, turned purple and looked like he might hit her.

That was when she realized that she'd seriously mis-judged Dunk. In superhero fashion, he was there in a flash, informing the customer that he had two choices, leave or chill in wet pants. Apparently word got around that 'Gin' wasn't open to earning tips the touchy feely way because there wasn't another incident.

Raze made it clear that he'd seen the whole thing, just by the way he stared at her. She took the fact that he said nothing to mean he approved or at least did not disapprove enough to make a deal out of it.

DEV MERIT HAD been thrown out of his SoCal MC, the Renegades. Or, to be fair, the officers had voted to transfer him rather than engage in a war with a rival. It seemed the enforcer of a rival club had a problem with Dev fucking his wife.

They gave him a choice of four clubs that would take him. He wasn't thrilled about any of them, but settled on the SSMC in Austin.

"And keep it in your pants when there's a ring on the bitch's finger." That was the goodbye comment from his former prez.

Dev couldn't help it if women competed for his attentions. It was a gift. He supposed he could be somewhat more discreet and he had thirteen hundred long miles to think that over on the way to Austin. He was just fifteen minutes away from the SSMC when he spotted a roadhouse in a little town called Dripping Springs.

He decided he'd stop in, have a bite, relieve himself, and get the local lay of the land before heading over to the Sanctuary compound.

Within seconds of stepping inside he spotted a group of three bikers in the corner. They were wearing SSMC colors. So he decided to introduce himself. They'd heard he was coming and were glad to get a new member with his particular skill set, which was custom bike design. Wrecks and Rides was always looking for talent, especially if it had a following.

They shook hands, kicked out a chair, and invited him to join them.

Dev had removed the patches from his jacket because it wasn't advisable to wear colors while riding alone and passing through the territories of at least eighteen clubs. But everything about his manner and dress screamed biker.

CLOVER QUICKLY LEARNED that wandering hands were not the only pitfall to serving at a roadhouse. There was also the sort of lechery that might be welcome under the right circumstances. Such was the case of the blond biker with the beautiful smile.

She noticed him join a table of guys who'd already been served. So she stopped by. "What will you have?"

He looked up and ran his eyes over her in a blatant, checking-you-out-and-you're-passing-with-flying-colors sort of way. Sparkling blue eyes that seemed to say, "I know something you don't," lingered on her breasts then shifted to scan her name tag. Smiling like the canary-eating cat, he said, "I'll have some of that," and pointed to the temporary label that read 'Gin'.

She didn't acknowledge the double meaning he surely intended. Instead, she returned his smile and said, "Coming up."

When she walked away, she could hear his friends laughing. Beautiful biker was stuck with what he would almost certainly view as a woman's drink. Gin.

AFTER TURNING ON the security system, they walked to Raze's house together.

"D'you do okay tonight?" he asked as they walked.

"I did. Better than last night. And it felt like I knew a little bit more about what I was doing."

He nodded. "That's good then. I'm just gonna grab some clothes for in the mornin'," he said. "Then I'll be out of your hair."

She nodded. "You know, that's silly. Putting you out of your own bed for a night was bad enough. Two is excessive. Let me just grab my duffel and I'll take the studio. Which I'm grateful to have access to," she added.

He put a hand on her elbow and stopped her. "When I get the lock fixed. Maybe tomorrow. Meantime, you stay here with Bless. The studio was built for me." He didn't go into the fact that it had actually been built for far-too-young newlyweds. "And I'll sleep sound as a baby." She hesitated. "I'll be right back."

He disappeared into his bedroom. As he went past he couldn't help notice that the bed was made any more than he could help noticing that a pair of jeans, a tee shirt, and a matching set of red lacy bra and panties were on the bed. Seeing the lingerie, apparently worn, on his bed did something to his nether regions. He went hard as a rock. That sort of spontaneous reaction had not been part of his reality for a very long time.

Checking over his shoulder to make sure he wasn't seen, he adjusted himself, stole another look, and opened a bureau drawer. He rushed straight for the door so that she wouldn't think it was strange that he was holding clothing in front of his crotch. Some guys could get away with random boners and not have attention focused like 'breaking news', but not Raze. Being extremely well endowed was a mixed blessing and unwanted attention was the downside of the mix.

"Lock this door behind me," he said, and hurried

out without waiting for a goodnight.

"Huh," she said to Bless before walking over and locking the door as instructed.

RAZE LAY ON his back on the bed that had been his growing up. It was an extra-long, dormitory style twin. So it still accommodated his height.

The roadhouse had performed to maximum profit potential. Raze & Ruin had been packed with paying customers who clearly had a fine time and would be back.

He was tired, but his mind was restless. It kept jumping from the dance and how the top of stray girl's head had come to his chin. How pleased she looked when she caught onto the dance steps. How surprised she'd looked when he'd smiled.

"Jesus," he said out loud to the darkness. He supposed he'd gotten used to talking to Bless and now just talked to no one. Like a crazy man.

He tried to keep his mind from returning to the red lacy lingerie, but he couldn't stop picturing how it had looked thrown aside on top of his own bed, or how it would look on stray girl with no other clothes on her incredible body. He'd watched her all night, graceful as a dancer, hips swaying, drawing the eyes of every man in the place. He liked that she was interesting to his customers, but hated when customers looked too long and too hard.

"What the fuck is wrong with me?" he said to the room.

Every time his thoughts returned to the bra and panties his erection got more insistent until he knew he was going to have to take care of it before going to sleep. He did, with a vision of stray girl dancing in red lingerie, partly angry about the borderline discomfort, partly pleased and relieved to know his dick was still working.

He drifted to sleep hoping that Press would not find what was wrong with the car.

CHAPTER EIGHT

THE CAR THAT WILL TAKE YOU AWAY FROM ME

U2 – *With or Without you*

CLOVER WOKE TO the smell of coffee. And bacon? She realized she must have been exhausted because she couldn't recall going to bed. If she moved during the night, it didn't wake her. She'd slept like the dead. But now there was coffee. And bacon.

After rushing through a quick shower, she pulled on torn jeans, a soft short sleeve tee, dabbed on light makeup, towel dried her hair and left it down.

"That smells too good to be true. Is there any bacon left?"

She couldn't help noticing how good Raze looked in jeans as he faced toward the stove and away from her.

Looking over his shoulder, he took her in from her

wet hair down to the poodle-pink nail polish on her bare toes, before saying, "Haven't touched it yet, sleepy. No point in makin' blueberry pancakes until you're up."

"Why?" she asked as she sidled close to where he was standing at the stove. "You don't like them? I know how to make them if you want me to take over. Not that it's not fun to have you do it."

"Well, then, sit yourself down at the table there and let me finish what I started."

"Yes, sir." She saluted. After pouring a cup of coffee, she said, "So the band last night was good, huh?"

"Yep. Folks like 'em."

"They did, but you were the star of the show."

His eyes slid to hers. "That's how you see it?"

She laughed. "That's how *everybody* saw it. All night long that's all I heard. Raze was amazing. Raze sure looked good out there with you."

"You're makin' this up."

"Am not." She jumped up to sit on the cabinet so she could see his face while she talked to him. "Those people seem to really like you. Care about you, I guess.

So it's a really small town?"

"Small enough that a lot of people know who I am. I wouldn't go so far as to say that they *'care'* about me. Most people stay pretty busy caring about themselves."

"Wow. That's pretty cynical."

"No. It's just real."

"Hmmm. You know what's not cynical?"

"What?"

"Taking in a perfect stranger. Giving her a job and dinner, letting her sleep in your bed, and talk to your dog."

He cocked his head. "You talk to my dog?"

Nodding, she said, "She's a great listener." He flipped a pancake onto her plate and handed it to her. She took the plate but didn't move. She just stared.

"What's wrong?"

She looked up at him with an expression that was undisguised admiration. "Nothing is wrong. This pancake is perfect. As in perfection. I mean it could be a model for a magazine shoot."

That finally broke his lugubrious resistance down to

the point where he could not help but emit a small chuckle. She jerked her face toward the sound, but he was already recomposed by that time.

"Want another?" he asked.

"Is that a trick question?"

"I take that as a yes."

"Take it as a hell yes."

"Alright then. This is a sit down breakfast. Have a seat at the table like a big girl." He put two pieces of bacon on the side of her plate.

"For another one of these," she said with a mouthful of blueberry pancake, "I'll sit anywhere you want."

She grimaced, realizing that her comment could be taken as a sexual reference, but anything she said in follow-up would only make it worse. So she sat down and went about quietly consuming heavenly pancakes.

"Have you talked to the mechanic?" She thought she saw Raze's shoulders stiffen slightly.

"He said he'd call," Raze said.

"I know. I just thought... Never mind."

"You eager to get on the road?"

"Eager to find out how much it will cost to get the hunk of junk running. For me, I mean. I know it's running for everybody else."

Raze slid another pancake onto her plate then sat down across from her. "Things are pretty quiet on Sunday nights," he said idly. "And we close at midnight."

"Oh? Does that mean you don't need me to work?"

"No. It means you can have the work, but don't expect to make as much."

"Okay." She shrugged. "So. No dancing?"

He ignored that and said, "We're closed tomorrow."

"Really?"

"Every Monday. If your car is ready, we can go get it."

She nodded. "Okay."

RAZE WAS RIGHT. Sunday nights were nothing like Friday and Saturday. There were some locals who used the roadhouse as their pub, apparently came in for drink and conversation every night. No live music. Not much activity in the kitchen.

She spent most of the time getting caught up on local gossip. Luke wasn't bartending, but Carl was. And Carl turned out to be a talker. She heard all the juicy on every RRR employee, but when she asked about Raze, she hit a barrier.

"Nuh-uh," Luke said. "Draw the line at tellin' tales about the bossman."

"Come on. Blur the line. I won't tell."

He was shaking his head with a smile before she finished the sentence. "Wild horses couldn't make me, sugar."

She came closer and whispered in a tone of conspiracy, "At least tell me if he has a girlfriend." She was more asking for confirmation than information. Since she was staying in his house, she had inside information already. She knew there were no photographs. Of anybody. And no hint that women were ever there. No feminine shampoo. No pink razors. No loofahs. Nada.

Carl's head-shaking became even more vigorous. "Don't know nothin' about Raze's personal life." Clover slumped a little. "But I've never seen him with anybody. Never seen him show an interest in anybody." He chuckled and looked at Clover pointedly. "Until last night." Then he leaned close. "Oh. And there's a rumor goin' 'round that a certain cutie pie is stayin' at his place."

Clover jerked back like she'd been bitten by a snake. When Carl laughed, her eyes flashed. "You'd better not be confirming any loose talk if you know what's good for you." She smiled evilly. "I know the boss."

His laughter died. His smile fell. And he got very busy at the bar.

SHE WALKED BACK to the house with Raze after he set the security system in what seemed to have become a routine.

"Just gettin' some clothes," he said.

"Maybe tomorrow we could see about a different lock? Um. For the studio?"

Raze stopped on his way to get a change of clothes. It was the first time the woman had talked in terms of a next day in Dripping Springs. Something about that sat right.

"Maybe."

Clover set the bedside alarm, determined to get up earlier and make coffee for Raze for a change. Maybe bacon and biscuits as well.

She was pulling biscuits out of the oven when she heard the key in the lock on the kitchen door and saw that Bless was turning in anxious circles, barely able to contain her excitement that Raze was home. When he stepped through the door, the dog's whines reached a loud and impossibly high pitch.

After giving the dog her due, Raze looked over at stray girl. "What's this?"

Something different, an expression she hadn't seen before passed over his face. It wasn't a smile, but the lines between his brows appeared to be less pronounced, his jaw wasn't quite as firmly set, and there was something in his eyes.

If Raze was somebody else, she would have said he

looked glad to see her, but Raze was Raze. Hard, if not impossible, to read. So she dismissed it as imagination or, God forbid, wishful thinking.

"Biscuits. Bacon." She waved at the stove. "I can make scrambled eggs? If you like?"

"I like scrambled eggs," he replied, seeming mildly pleased.

Raze poured himself a cup of coffee, glanced at stray girl, and shuffled over to have a seat at the dinette where he could see every inch of the kitchen and every inch of the occupants in the kitchen.

His only day off, which was rarely an actual day off, wasn't starting off the way he'd imagined. He'd prepared to let himself into the house, feed and water his dog, then make breakfast for himself and the mystery woman who'd been occupying his bed for two nights. Without him in it.

He expected to open the door to Bless turning in circles doing her best to say she was *thrilled* to see him. He did not expect the vision of stray girl bent over at the waist to bring a sheet of giant heavenly smelling biscuits out of the oven. Desire for the biscuits went straight through his nose and aroused his hunger, making him practically salivate. Desire for the woman went straight through his eyes to his cock and aroused his hunger, making him practically want to salivate.

She opened the refrigerator to pull out the carton of eggs from the lowest shelf, which caused Raze to shift in his chair and surreptitiously shift the package to a somewhat less uncomfortable angle. But there was something more than the sexual interest his body was expressing for hers.

The kitchen felt different. The whole house felt different. She changed the energy in drastic ways and amplified the feeling of aliveness. He even felt different about waking up in the morning.

Bless had brought him a long way back toward the living. Stray girl, whether she knew it or not, was dragging him across the finish line and he was putting up less resistance with each minute that passed.

The eggs were ready in five minutes. Clover didn't ask what Raze would like or how much. She put bacon, eggs, and biscuits on a plate, set it in front of him, and said, "There's more if you want. We don't have any jam, but there's butter. For your biscuits."

"That'd be nice," he said, noticing that she used the pronoun 'we' when describing the food stores in his kitchen. He checked in with himself to see if that bothered him and found, surprisingly, that it did not. He was sure it was just verbal shorthand and cautioned himself not to read anything into it.

She moved the butter from the counter by the stove to the table.

When she made no move to get a plate for herself, Raze said, "You're not gonna join me?"

"Oh," she said, like she'd momentarily forgotten where she was and what she was doing. "Yes. I am."

She put food on a plate for herself, sat down, and smiled at the man who was nibbling on a bacon strip.

"It's weird to eat breakfast at noon, isn't it?" she said.

"You get used to it."

"I guess."

"So about today…"

"Uh-huh?"

"I'm gonna take Bless for a run."

"Okay."

"Then we can ride over and see how Press is comin' on your car if you like."

She smiled. "Sure. It's not like I've got anything to do. I mean, here I am in the Outback with no transportation." When she stopped talking she realized that didn't come out right.

He studied her while he ate half a biscuit. When he swallowed he said, "You do know this is not the 'Outback'. Right?"

"Yes. Of course I know that. I just meant…"

"Yeah. I think I know what you meant." He watched her carefully as he said, "You meant that you're used to being in a place so far away from here that everything about our way of life is alien to you. A metropolis. Teeming with people." Even he could read the signals when her face and manner instantly sobered. She put her fork down and sat up straight, which looked a lot like a defensive posture. So he decided it was time to change the subject. "Anyway. We'll go see about your car. Maybe go for a ride in the hill country. Have some Mexican food."

Her lips moved ever so slightly, like the smile was threatening to return.

"Sound good?" he asked.

She nodded. "Yeah. And the lock."

"We'll see."

WHILE RAZE AND Bless were gone, she cleaned up, put on pink sneakers with ribbon laces, applied some light makeup, made the bed, arranged her stuff in piles on the floor next to the duffel then turned on the TV. Halfway through a Lifetime movie about a woman unwittingly living with a sicko killer she heard the kitchen door open and close.

Bless came padding into the room panting.

"Hello. Good workout?" Bless raised her head fleetingly, quirked her eyebrows then looked away. "Don't want to talk about it, huh? I get that. Subject closed."

Bless flopped down in one of the several dog beds scattered around the house, that one in front of a low window where she could look out and keep watch while resting her chin on the windowsill.

Half an hour later Raze came in fresh from a shower with hair damp at the ends.

"You ready?" he said.

"No! I can't leave now." Other than glancing up when he came in, Clover didn't seem able to take her eyes away from the TV.

Raze walked over, picked up the remote, hit record, then turned it off.

"What are you doing!?!" She sounded as incredulous as if he'd just turned into a werewolf right in front of her.

"Relax. It's recorded. You can watch the rest later."

She looked from him to the TV and back again and decided that was okay. Standing she said, "I guess I'm ready then."

She followed him out to the free-standing garage, which she supposed he never used, because the truck was always parked under the adjacent carport between the garage and the house. He used a remote in his pocket to open the door and she followed him in to where a very large and very shiny black and chrome Harley sat in the middle of the room looking like a museum exhibit.

When he handed her the helmet to put on, she started shaking her head. "No. No. No. No. No. Look, Ruin. You made me wait tables when I had no idea how to do it. Didn't even know what 'steak fingers' were. You made me do that Louisiana dance in front of everybody in the world even though I didn't know how and looked like an idiot. You made me put the Cheetos back in the store. But I draw the line at this. I am absolutely positively for sure *not* getting on this thing. Not ever in this lifetime."

His response was to take her face between both big hands and teach her the meaning of being kissed stupid. He reveled in the little gasp that was an involuntary statement of what he took to be both surprise and excitement.

Raze was right on both counts.

Surprised.

And excited.

She didn't resist when he pulled her in. How could she? Her mind went blank. There was something about his smell that was an intoxicant, not to mention an accelerant. During the space of the full minute he was staking a quit deed claim to her mouth, Clover realized that her entire history of sexual encounter had been with boys. A series of boys. Minute by minute Raze was teaching her that her experience was irrelevant. Because he was a man. Hardened. Experienced. And accustomed to being large and in charge.

When he was finally satisfied that he'd kissed the protest out of her, he pulled back. Stray girl's eyes were closed and she was swaying on her feet. He kept hold of her just to be sure she didn't fall over. When she opened her eyes, he searched them, first one then the other.

She had no idea what he was trying to find there, but she supposed that had answered her inner question about whether or not he was exceptionally kind to the homeless, or interested in her – in *that* way.

Raze didn't know what it was about mystery girl that caused his body to do impulsive things without first checking in with his brain. It was weird. Unsettling. And exciting all at the same time.

"Trust me," he said. "You're gonna love it."

TEN MINUTES LATER they were speeding north on 169 on the way to the SSMC compound. Stray girl was wearing the helmet he'd insisted on and had a death grip around Raze's waist. He was shocked to realize he was smiling. He didn't know if that was because of the ride, the woman whose arms were threatening to cut off his air, or the kiss. He decided he didn't care. Moments of smiling for no reason had been in short supply in his life in the past few years. So he knew to appreciate such things if they turned his way.

The next moment, when he realized he was smiling about a woman who was a complete mystery, who hadn't so much as divulged her last name, his smile fell and the worry lines between his brows resumed their post. He couldn't let himself fall for somebody who was obviously running from something. And, judging by the way she clammed up whenever innocent questions were posed, the something she was running from was more than likely shit that was leagues deep. He had to either find out what he was getting into or cut her loose. And he had to do it that very day, before he spent another fitful night with visions of red lacy lingerie. Before Bless started to get too attached.

That, of course, was his way of saying before *he* got too attached.

SITTING BEHIND THE wheel of her car with the window rolled down, she listened while the mechanic named Press talked to Raze.

He was shaking his head. "I don't get it. Never been stumped like this. Just on the off chance that it really is some out there mumbo jumbo thing, I had Garland and Brigid get in and start it when they were here. So it's not that the car doesn't like women." He glanced her way. "It's just her."

That caused Raze to look her way as well. "Okay," he said. "If you need to pull it around back until I can get it picked up... Do what you need to. I'm gonna try to get her money back. Get her somethin' else."

Clover's ears perked up. *He was?*

"Sorry, man," Press said. "This is one for the books."

"Yeah. Thanks for tryin'."

Raze took her hand and pulled her out of the Toyota. "Let's go. I'm gonna show you somethin' cool then we'll get some Mexican. Everything seems better with bean and cheese nachos smothered in jalapenos."

She blinked. "Jalapenos? I don't think so. Are you really going to get my money back?"

She was looking at him like he was some kind of knight in armor going on a quest for a lady. And fuck if he didn't like that look. "Gonna try. How much you give him?"

"Seven twenty-five."

He nodded. "See what I can do."

"Thank you." She was grateful that he was going to make an effort to help her out. She was also relieved that he didn't bend over laughing claiming that she'd been taken by a local barely-out-of-teens con artist.

"You can thank me if I hand you the cash. Until then, it's just an idea."

"Still."

"You like the last word, don't ya?"

She smiled. "Everybody likes the last word, Ruin."

As she was climbing on behind Raze, Arnold was coming toward the hangar.

"That a woman on the back of your bike, Killer?"

Raze looked at Arnold. "Time to get your eyeglass prescription checked if you need to ask that question."

"Y'all have a nice day." Arnold smiled like the Cheshire cat.

"Fuck you," Raze said just loud enough for Arnold to hear.

Arnold walked away chuckling and lifting his hand in a dismissive wave.

RAZE RODE STRAIGHT to Pedernales State Park and stopped overlooking one of thousands of limestone formations. That one made natural stair step terraces down to the river. Since it was a Monday afternoon, there was nobody else around.

"I've never seen water that color before," she said. "Emerald green."

"You like water? I mean gettin' in it?"

She shrugged. "Well, sure."

"Lots of places around here to swim or tube or just get wet. Just sayin' that, if you end up stickin' around, there's stuff to do."

She smiled at that, liking the fact that Raze was trying to sell her on Dripping Springs.

"I hear there's also this great little roadhouse. Live music. Good food."

He nodded and slid his eyes sideways. "Nice things to look at."

She grinned. "And the owner puts on a nightly floor show."

His mouth practically contorted trying not to smile, but eventually he surrendered to it, which made her laugh. And appreciate the appearance of the gorgeous boyish smile that took years away from his face and made her heart alternate between fluttering and trying to stop.

"That was a One. Time. Thing."

"Uh-huh," she teased. "They say that, once performers get a taste of the attention, they can't quit it. It's like an addiction."

He snorted and brought the Harley roaring to life. "Hold on," he said.

SITTING OUTSIDE ON the deck at Chuy's, they ate nachos, though Clover scraped the jalapenos off hers through looks of incredulity and disdain from her companion. Then she stuffed herself with chicken flautas and stole one of Raze's shrimp tacos.

Raze had never had anyone take food from his plate before. He thought he ought to resent it, or think it was rude or not ladylike, but he didn't think those things. Goddamn if he didn't kind of like it.

"I'm so full I can barely move," she said as she swung her leg over the bike again.

"You don't need to move. Just hold on tight. I'll do the moving."

That was not a problem. She liked leaning against his back and the pleasure of pressing her arms around his tight abs counterbalanced the fright of the ride.

Back at Raze's house, she said, "You want to come in for a beer?"

He didn't laugh outwardly but did think being invited inside his own house to drink one of his own beers was funny. He unlocked the door and held it open for her. "Go watch the rest of your show. I got an errand."

"Okay."

IT DIDN'T TAKE long for Raze to learn that Henry was out of work and shacked up with a girlfriend who worked the drive-through at the Dairy Queen. They lived in a two-story apartment that had seen much better days. The best thing that could be said about it was that it was located on the edge of the Walmart parking lot.

Raze made a fist and banged on the door with the

side of his hand.

"Who is it?" a voice said from inside.

"Open up, Henry. Need to talk for a second."

When Henry cracked the door open, Raze pushed his way in.

"What the fu…?"

"Who is this, Hen?" Dairy Queen interrupted, raising her voice to be heard above the noise of the soap opera she was watching.

"I don't have business with you," Raze told her. "So stay out of this."

The girl closed her mouth.

Raze turned back to Henry. "You sold a woman a car couple of days ago."

"Yeah? So?"

"It won't start for her. I'm gonna be needin' that money back."

Henry's eyes widened. "There was nothin' wrong with that car. It was a good sale. Fair to both of us."

"So you say. But the fact is that it won't start for her. Got the best mechanic I know to go over it."

"What is she to you?"

"That's none of your business, Henry. It's not an answer either. Just get me the money and I'll give you the address where you can pick up the car."

"I cain't give that money, Raze. It's spent."

"On what?"

"Got Millie a ring."

Raze looked at Millie, who proudly held up an engagement ring with a diamond so tiny that location would require a magnifying glass.

"Congratulations," Raze said drily. "You're gonna need to take it back and get a refund so you can repay the lady you gypped."

"I cain't do that, Raze. We got the ring over at All Star Pawn. And you know they don't give money back."

Raze stared at Henry for a few seconds. The kid was right. All Star Pawn was a black hole. Cash that went in didn't come out again.

Without another word he walked out and left the door standing open just because it was a menacing shit move and he was in a bad mood. He straddled his bike and pulled the phone out.

"'Lo, brother," Brash said when he answered.

"Brash, I'm lookin' for a favor. Actually two."

"Name it."

"That car I left at the club."

"Yeah?"

"Need you to sell it for me. Don't care if it's for parts. I also need to buy somethin' to replace it. Somethin' clean. Dependable."

Brash didn't try to hide the smile in his voice. "Suitable for a woman."

"Yeah," Raze said slowly.

"How much you lookin' to pay?"

"I don't know. Three maybe. No more."

"Just so happens, the club owns part of a used car establishment."

"I am not surprised. Where is it?"

"South Austin. Ben White."

"They take credit cards?"

Brash snorted. "Raze. If an outfit does not take credit cards, they are out of business."

"Okay. Sittin' on my bike under a tree. Waitin' right here."

"Nah. Go on and head on over there. I'll meet you. We'll find somethin' that works. It's just inside the loop. Forty-seven hundred."

"See ya there."

Brash was only ten minutes away from the car lot. He wrapped up his appointment, headed over, and, by the time Raze pulled in, Brash had come to an understanding with the owner.

Raze backed his bike into a spot by the office door and walked over to where Brash was waiting by a cherry-looking-red 2006 Jeep Liberty Sport. Cute as cute could be. It also happened to be the same color as a set of lacy lingerie he couldn't seem to forget about.

"What d'ya think?" Brash smiled.

"I think that's a long way from the three thousand we talked about."

"I happen to know that you could afford to buy a Rolls if you wanted one."

"That's not the point. The point is that she needs to

think I got her a replacement for the seven hundred twenty-five dollars she paid for that piece of shit."

"Oh." Brash nodded, not even trying to contain his delight that Raze was car shopping for a woman. "Well it's a good thing this car fits the bill. And it can be yours today, right now, for the low, low price of two thousand nine hundred ninety-nine dollars. Tax, title, license included."

Raze narrowed his eyes. "That's impossible."

Brash shook his head. "Nothin's impossible when you know the right people. So happens the owner got a deal on this vehicle and, as part owner, we're waiving the profit."

Raze's lips parted when he started to let himself imagine taking that car back to stray girl. He began looking the car over in earnest. If there was a scratch or dent, he didn't see it. It was fully loaded with a rear mount spare and ivory leather that had been maintained. Soft, supple, without a tear.

Raze popped the hood. "D'you drive it?"

"No. Figured you'd want to. It has a hundred and

twenty-seven thousand miles on it, but it's in good shape and you got the chops to keep it runnin' for years."

Raze was apparently satisfied with what he saw under the hood. Brash held up his hand and a guy in a short-sleeved white button-down threw him the keys, which he handed to Raze.

The two of them took the car for a spin on the loop and gave it the sort of test drive that would give a car dealer apoplexy. But they were satisfied the Jeep would meet stray girl's needs.

When they pulled back in, Raze turned off the car and looked at Brash. "It's perfect. Guess I owe you one. Again."

"You owe me nothin'." Then he chuckled. "But before we sell that Toyota, seems like we ought to call in a gypsy or a medium, find out what's the deal."

Raze smiled, which shocked Brash down to his biker boots. "You should," he agreed. "Though I gotta say, whatever it was, I might be just as glad that car refused to take her away."

Brash grinned as he got out. "Finish up the paper, Charlie," he called to the guy in the white shirt.

"Charge me extra for delivery. I need somebody to drive it over to my place."

"I'll drive. Charlie's got a bobtail and a ramp. We'll put your bike in the truck. I'll drive the truck, haul your bike, and bring it back."

"One condition. Bring the whole club for Bike Night. Beer and wings on the roadhouse. Wives, too."

Brash grinned. "On behalf of the club, that is an offer I cannot refuse. Thursday night. We will be there. Who's playin'? Not that it matters."

"Thunder."

"Excellent."

"Whose name do you want me to put on the paperwork?" Charlie asked.

Raze answered. "Just sign it over and leave the new owner blank."

CLOVER WAS TOO engrossed in another Lifetime movie to hear the truck pull up outside. She thought she might have heard the clank of metal, but it didn't sound threatening so she stayed where she was.

It took both men to get Raze's seven-hundred-pound Harley down the ramp and out of the truck. He parked it in the garage, pulled the door down, and walked over to shake Brash's hand.

"Aw. You're not gonna let me see her reaction?" Raze looked like a deer in headlights. "Just kiddin'. The moment is all yours. See you Thursday."

"Thanks again."

"Don't mention it."

"Speaking of that. Don't..." he glanced toward the house, "tell her anything about..."

Brash looked offended. "I won't! Christ, Raze. I didn't just find the boys' club yesterday."

Raze nodded and offered a tiny smile, which was all the thanks Brash needed.

CHAPTER NINE

CONFESSIONAL

Bruce Springsteen – *Cover Me*

"YOU HERE?" RAZE yelled from the kitchen door. Of course he knew she was there. First, he could hear the TV. Second, where else would she be? But he wanted to warn her, as a courtesy, and not alarm her by walking in unexpectedly.

"Yeah," she hollered.

He stepped into the living room and glanced at the TV. "You at a stoppin' point? Got somethin' I want to show you."

"What?" She brightened and looked as excited as a child at the mention of ice cream.

He gave her the tiniest lopsided grin. "Just come."

"Okay." She used the remote to turn off the TV, slid

on her Vans, and shuffled over to where he stood. "Am I going to like it?"

"Hope so."

He'd parked the car sideways on the gravel drive at the end of the walkway that led to the carport and garage. He opened the kitchen door and stepped back so that she could go through first.

When she saw the car, she said, "Is somebody here?"

"No. It's yours."

She looked confused. "What's mine?"

"The car, silly."

She gaped, mouth moving, but no sound coming out. "That's not my car. That car is gorgeous. And new. And... perfect."

He was nodding. "Yeah. It is all that. It's also yours."

She looked up at Raze with liquid eyes. "How?"

"Went over to Henry's and asked for your money back. Then I called in a favor. Got you a car worth havin'. It's in good shape. It'll last a long time."

Overwhelmed didn't begin to describe the emotions

that were churning in her brain and in her stomach. People didn't go out of their way to make things easier for her. Quite the opposite, it seemed.

"I don't know what to say, Ruin. It's just… so perfect," she repeated.

"Say, 'Let's go for a drive'."

She laughed. "Let's go for a drive!"

She started to climb in behind the steering wheel, but Raze said, "Don't you want to get your license?"

Stopping dead still, she realized that he'd said she needed to get her license, not that he wanted to see it. "Sure." She smiled.

She grabbed her purse and, on the way to the back door, decided that Bless would like a ride, too. So she grabbed the leash, fastened it onto Bless's collar, and hurried back out to what she was sure was the best car in the world.

Bless jumped into the back seat.

"How did you know I like Jeeps?"

He smiled. "I didn't. How could I know that, stray girl?"

"I think it's a sign."

"A sign of what?"

She shrugged. "Have I ever told you I love red?" she asked Raze.

He shook his head slightly. "No. You never have."

Taking a deep breath before she turned the key, she looked at Raze as if to say, "Will it or won't it?"

The car growled awake then settled into a pleasant purr. She laughed and rolled the back window down for Bless.

Raze couldn't remember if he'd ever felt more pleasure than he got from watching stray girl's delight. She was practically glowing. Now and then she would stop and fiddle with something on the console or the steering column. She tried the radio, the cruise control, and the fog lights.

"Oh look. This shows me what direction I'm going." She was referring to a small lighted directional display on the rear view mirror.

"It doesn't have GPS."

"I don't need that. I have this!" She tapped the little

display on the mirror that said NW.

"It is four wheel drive. That means you're gonna spend more in gas, but you're not likely to get stuck in the mud."

She nodded her approval. "The inside feels like, I don't know, luxury. I don't know how you got this for… Wait a minute. Did somebody die in this car?"

Raze stared at her for a full two seconds before laughter overtook him. Since Clover had never heard him laugh before, she was momentarily stunned.

She pulled off to the side of the road and said, "That's the first time I've heard you laugh." He shrugged. "Tell me why that is."

"What? That I'm not yucking it up half the time like a damn fool?"

"No," she said carefully. "Why you're so serious *most* of the time. Did something bad happen to you?"

Looking into her eyes, in the quiet intimacy of the cab of a Jeep Liberty, he felt like he could lose himself in the sincerity he read there. Of its own volition, his hand reached over to slide a lock of silky hair through his fingers. It was cool to the touch. And soft. So soft. He was a little mesmerized by the feel.

At length he said, "I guess to answer that question I'd have to tell you stuff about myself."

"Okay."

"You think you could find your way back to the house?"

She looked around and laughed when she realized that she was going to have to admit that she had no idea where they were. She shook her head.

"Let's head back. Turn left at that stop sign."

Six minutes later they were walking into the kitchen. She sat down at the dinette. Raze put an envelope of papers on the table before he went to the refrigerator and took out a beer. He held up a bottle in query as to whether she wanted one or not.

She said, "Water. Please."

When he sat down, he opened the envelope and took out the papers. "I had them leave the name blank since I'm not sure what name is on your driver's license. And it needs to match. Right now the car has an insurance binder in my name. We'll get it switched over as soon as I know who to say is the owner of the car."

She looked down and put her hands in her lap. "Please don't think I'm not grateful for... everything. But I can't tell you any more about me than I already have."

"What is it that you think might happen if you talk to me? About whatever it is that's going on?"

"Well..." The truth was that, a couple of days before, when she hadn't known anything about him, she didn't know if he was the sort of person who would try to claim a reward. But even though she acknowledged that she wasn't always the world's best judge of character, hence three ex-boyfriends and one ex-husband, she felt sure down to the curl of her toes that Raze Rouen was not the betraying kind. "Would you promise that anything I say...?"

"Just between us. You got my word."

"I'm not telling stuff that could get me killed to somebody who won't say why he doesn't smile."

"I smile." His response was automatic while his

brain was still replaying the phrase 'get me killed'.

"No. You don't. I spent the first few hours working for you calling you 'frowny guy'. And here's the thing. *Everybody* knew who I was talking about."

"That might have been because of the context."

"No. It wasn't because of the context, Ruin. It was because they only see you frown."

He took a swig of beer, eyes never leaving hers. "Woman wrecked my life."

When he didn't say more, she said, "Really? I'm not seeing that. Your life looks pretty together to me. You've got a thriving business. You own your own house. Two vehicles. A dog who'd die for you. Friends who like you enough to make an event out of teasing you. And a community who practically cheers when they see you dance. Your life doesn't look *wrecked*. It looks like one big fat success story."

Hearing things from an objective perspective caused an almost instantaneous shift. She was right. Dead on. And damn. What was he acting so fucking miserable about?

She wasn't done. "But I still want to hear the story."

"Why?"

"Because I like you and, if you feel like your life was ruined," she couldn't help but stop and smile at the play on words, "I want to know what you're thinking. Wait. That's not right. I'd want to know your history no matter what."

"I'll give the pocket version if you swear you'll tell me everything and not hold back." She looked solemn, like she wasn't down with the plan. "The car is gassed up. All you have to do is fill your name in on the paperwork. I'll give you what you earned for three shifts in addition to your tips. You can drive away and not look back.

"Or you can hang around long enough to see where this goes." He motioned between the two of them, like it had been established that there was a 'them' to factor in. "I need to know who's sleeping in my bed. And why." He sat back and stretched his long legs out in front of him. "That's not too much to ask. I probably don't have to tell you how I'm hopin' you choose, but if I got you a car that's gonna take you away from me… so be it. I can't get in deeper without knowin' who you are."

Clover put both palms to her cheeks and blinked several times, thinking she could be making the best decision or the worst mistake of her life. "Alright. Deal."

"Deal, you'll tell me everything?"

"Yes."

It didn't take long for Raze to describe his history. How he'd been dumped with his uncle, why he'd joined the Guard and ended up in a war zone, the cheating, the divorce, everything. He expected stray girl to be sympathetic and feel sorry for him. If she did, that was not what she said.

What she said was, "You lied to me."

"What?"

"I said 'you're not an expert on car mechanics' and you didn't deny it. And it turns out you're like the great kowabunga of all grease monkeys."

Slowly he smiled. "You didn't ask me if I knew anything about cars."

"A subtle distinction."

"No. It's not. I also didn't tell you that I like Wagner. That doesn't mean I lied about it."

She frowned at the incongruity of that statement. "You like German opera?" He shrugged, looked away, and turned the bottle up. She watched the movement of his throat as he swallowed. Fascinating. "Then you also lied about ignorance of *Lord of the Rings*. I'd bet on it!"

He might have looked a tiny bit sheepish. "Fine. You got me there. I have read *Lord of the Rings*. Saw the movies, too." He waved toward the living room. "On cable."

"Well," she said, "that invalidates our deal. I can't tell my story to a liar."

The gleam that jumped to Raze's eyes made him look like he was channeling the devil himself. Clover instantly began reconsidering the wisdom of teasing the devil. Himself. "You think you can break a deal with a man like me?"

When he began to stand slowly, she said, "Eeep," and bolted for the other room. It was a small house. She ran to the bedroom and tried to shut the door, but he was too fast. The door was torn out of her hands and a second later she found herself on her back on the bed being tickled mercilessly by a man who meant business and was clearly enjoyment her torment.

"Stop!" she panted breathlessly. "You can't do this."

He nodded decisively, white teeth making a rare appearance as he sat on top of her, legs straddling her hips. "I can. And I'm betting I can do this longer than you can do that."

She supposed what he meant by 'that' was squirming, gasping, turning purple, desperately trying and failing to get her midsection away from his hands.

"Please," she begged.

A charged current of sexual awareness slammed into both of them at the same time as the compromising nature of their surroundings and the electrical currents running between the touchpoints of their bodies simultaneously crystalized into a moment of perfect carnal clarity. Raze saw in her eyes that she would be his for the taking. And, while that might be a bucket list item, it was not on his immediate agenda. So he decided to steer things in a different direction before there was no turning back.

He stood up. Taking her hand, he pulled her to her feet and said, "Get your ass to the table. The kitchen is now your confessional. And I'm your fucking priest."

"LET'S START WITH your name."

"Clover."

Raze didn't know what he'd been expecting, but it hadn't been 'Clover'. He appeared to be attempting to marshal patience. "Is. That. Your. Real. Name?"

She shot out of her chair and stomped away to the bedroom. Each time her foot struck on the old wood floor forcefully he heard a slight rattle of dishes in the cabinets and felt the reverberation through his chair.

He looked at Bless, who was lying on the floor, but alert and keenly interested in whatever was disturbing the new pack member.

After the sounds of distant rustling from the other part of the small house, the sound of stomping reversed. She stormed back into the kitchen and slapped her driver's license down on the table.

"No need to be haughty," he said calmly. "It's not like I have no reason to be distrustful."

"You have NO reason to be distrustful. Other than my name I never told you one thing about myself, true or untrue."

His eyes cast downward to the license sitting on the table. He picked it up. Though not particularly flattering, it was a photo of the woman he knew as stray girl.

"Clover Fields." His eyes raised to hers slowly.

She rolled her eyes, threw her hands up, and let them fall on her thighs. "What can I say? My parents think they're funny. 'No one will forget your name, Clover. If you want to run for president of your class, you're halfway there because everybody will know you.'"

Raze sighed. "That's probably true. So your name is Clover Fields. It may take me a minute to get used to that."

"I don't want you to get used to it. You *cannot* use my name!"

Raze didn't bother to ask the question that was hanging in the air between them. "Why not?" simply didn't need to be said out loud.

Taking in and letting out a big breath, she gushed out the whole story like a fountain that had been clogged and was suddenly freed. She included the cheating husband and the credit card debt because she felt like she owed him the whole picture or nothing.

When she was done, he said, "Christ."

With a sigh, she said, "I think I'll take that beer now."

"How much was it?"

"The mob money? Two hundred and seventy-five thousand." He whistled. "Tell me about it. I was all set to be a slave to banks for the rest of my life. Then I thought I got a visit from a fairy godmother. That turned into an unwanted visit from the godfather."

"So your plan was to run to Texas? 'Cause you thought we don't have paved roads and telephones?"

"No! I didn't think that. I just thought it would be, you know, remote."

"So you bought a junker from Henry. Where were you gonna go?"

"I'd planned to keep going west." She stopped abruptly and focused on Raze. "Where would you have gone? If you were in, um, a situation like mine?"

Cocking his head, he said, "All things considered, I think I'd probably head to Cajun country."

"Louisiana?"

"Yeah. I learned somethin' about the culture when I was there with the Guard." He shrugged. "Lots of places to get lost. And with their history, Cajuns have gotten real good about mindin' their own business. Understandably. And keepin' things to themselves." He took a sip of beer and set the bottle down. "God willin', I'll never have to make a choice like that. But if I did, I'd head toward Lafayette Parish." He shifted his gaze to study Clover. "Smart of you to try to erase your cyber footprint. But if you ever got pulled over, they'd run your driver's license through the system."

"I didn't think of that."

"That's 'cause you're not a criminal, sugar. Lucky

for you, you found your way to Dripping Springs and then got stranded by a piece of shit Toyota." He chuckled and shook his head. "That apparently will start for anybody at all but you."

"That's not really funny," she said.

"Yeah." He smiled broader. "It is."

Raze got quiet and seemed lost in his head.

"What are you thinking?" she said.

Instantly his focus cleared as his eyes jerked to hers. "That it would be wrong to sell that car for parts." He pulled out his phone and called Brash. "Changed my mind. Don't sell that car." Pause. "Yeah. The one at the compound." Pause. "I don't know. That's the best I got." Pause. "Okay. Thanks." Pause. His gaze fixed on the woman patiently trying to figure out what was going on. "Yeah. She loves it. Fits her like a glove."

When he hung up, Clover looked resigned and her tone was flat. "You're giving me back the Toyota and sending me on my way." She sucked in a shaky breath, nodded resolutely, and started to rise. "That's what I…"

"Sit your butt right back down in that chair. You're

not goin' anywhere, 'cause we're a long way from done."
She sat back down, lines forming between her brows.
"Of course I'm not givin' you back the Toyota and
sendin' you on your way. What's the matter with you?
Are you daft? Or do you think I'm the kind of man who
runs from trouble?"

"But you said... about the car..." She pulled back,
looking confused as could be.

It wasn't so much that he wanted to avoid the appearance of sentimentality like a bad rash as that the
subject of the weird Toyota was off topic. At least that
was the line of logic followed by his inner rationaliza-
tion.

"I decided I want that car. End of story. It's for me.
Not for you. Why would I give you back a car that you
can't turn on? So you can live in the parking lot?"

"Well..."

"Well, I wouldn't. That's just silly."

"Okay." When put like that, it did seem to have
been a silly conclusion.

"Back to the matter at hand. This is one of those

things that can't be outrun. We've got to find a way to fix it. Permanently."

When his words began to sink in, she stared at him and blinked.

"We?" His eyes caught the tiny tremble of her bottom lip. The question he read on her face broke his heart in two. And that was *before* a single tear spilled out of her very expressive and, at the moment, very liquid eyes. The memory of the first time he ever saw her jumped to the screen of his mind. Damp. Lost. *And looking back over her shoulder.*

Stray girl was right. Bad stuff had come his way, but he'd always had a home. And even when he pushed them away, he knew he had friends who would drop everything in the middle of their own wedding and come if he asked them to.

The fact that she so desperately needed somebody on her side only made him determined to be that man. He'd use every resource in his arsenal, but he would see the day when Clover Fields never felt like she had to look back over her shoulder.

He leaned over, cupped her cheek with his big hand, and wiped the tear away with his thumb. Reflexively, she leaned into his hand. He liked the look and feel of that and knew that what he wanted out of life was for stray girl's impulse to always be movement *toward* him. Not away from him.

Leaning back, he said, "If providence was gonna dump you someplace, you're lucky that it was here. Because if you're runnin' from somethin', you couldn't be in a better place, except maybe a top secret bunker. And who wants to live like that? I've got resources. Friends who are as connected in their own way as the people you're crossways with."

He also had the money to clear her debt and knew that would be the quickest cleanest way to dispense with the problem.

CHAPTER TEN

BOUNTY HUNTER

Genesis – Just a Job to Do

T HIBAUT LE COCQ liked to keep a low profile in every way, including looks. He was six feet tall, medium build, with regular features. Not model handsome. Not unattractive. He wore his hair buzzed, no jewelry, no tattoos. When he was home in the south, he wore jeans, blue work shirts, boots, and baseball caps. When he was in other parts of the country, he wore jeans, boots, and Henleys. If he was traveling internationally, he adjusted accordingly.

Everything about his choice in style was designed to *not* call attention to himself. The less notice he attracted, the better. His regular looks formed the perfect disguise for a soul that was deformed and, for whatever reason, never fully developed.

Le Cocq was a Cajun bounty hunter out of Bon Aubry in the heart of Lafayette Parish, who worked both sides of the law. There was only one ideal that he was fully committed to. Personal profit accumulated by any means.

So he worked for bail bondsmen when they presented the easiest target with the greatest reward. As an equal opportunity freelancer, he would just as soon accept criminal patronage when it was convenient and a job caught his interest.

Only one policy stood between him and a hunt. He delivered whoever he was asked to run down, without fail. But he delivered them alive.

Thibaut Le Cocq was not a hitman. Not because he had qualms about dispatching people who, more than likely, had it coming, but because there was no point in taking on that jeopardy when he could earn what he wanted without the risk of prison time.

Sometimes Le Cocq's targets were delivered a little worse for wear. That was covered in his standard contract. But they were *always* alive.

He kept a home base in Bon Aubry, but was light on his feet. No ties that would hamper his ability to travel anywhere, anytime. Nothing to stand in the way of pursuing whatever job appeared to meet his qualifications. The qualification list was short. Lucrative and easy.

He liked easy.

Over a decade he'd earned a reputation for success and was a recipient of the daily update that arrived in a hushmail account. He'd reached a stature in his profession so that he vetted clients, not the other way around.

He got regular notices from bail bondsmen. He got less regular notices about jobs outside the usual channels. Those were always worth a look because they paid more, required zero paperwork, and he didn't have to maintain a license in the state where the prey was suspected to have fled.

HE'D BEEN HOME for less than a day after chasing a runner from D.C. to Panama then Ecuador before finally grabbing him in Venezuela. There was a week's worth of paper before the U.S. embassy decided to have Le Cocq complete extradition instead of using their own resources. He'd collected enough from that job to kick back and watch General Hospital for a couple of years, but after half a day, he was getting restless.

A 'concerned' New Jersey family was offering a hundred k for the 'safe' return of a missing person named Clover Fields. He sneered because it was obviously either an alias or a stripper name.

Unlike bail bonds notices, the 'flyer' didn't say what she did, but that was okay because he didn't care. A phone number was listed, which he knew would be a burner. Using his own disposable phone, he called to get the info.

The woman was reputed to be twenty-three. Clover Fields was her real name. *Huh.* She'd picked up a bag of cash that had been stashed in the wrong gym locker. When the rightful owner asked for the return of the money, she'd fled.

Le Cocq didn't care about any of that and was moderately bored with the details, but he listened and didn't interrupt, since the guy hiring him seemed talkative.

"What else?"

"Parents deceased. She has a much older sister who moved to Canada and became a citizen. No current love interest. Friends don't know where she went. She hasn't been in touch."

"I'll do it on an exclusive basis."

There was silence on the other end of the call. "I don't know if we can agree to that."

"Those are my terms. A hundred k and exclusivity. If I don't deliver in two weeks, you're free to open it up."

"Exclusivity for two weeks. Okay. Call me on this phone when you have her. I'll give you delivery instructions."

Le Cocq hung up, sat down at his desk, and opened a new file.

In addition to specialized search techniques, he had a network of plugged in informers all over the world. Each one knew that a good tip would result in an anonymous deposit to their Paypal account.

Within an hour he had the basics. College degree paid for with loans that would give Warren Buffet pause. Landed a nothing job at a barely solvent magazine that barely paid for her crap studio apartment. She was so squeaky clean she had never even been disciplined for smoking in high school.

From what his employer had told him, she'd left her crap car at her crap apartment and disappeared.

That kind of girl would not be able to figure out how to acquire an alternate identity. In the twenty-first century that meant no air travel. No ID. No fly.

That left train travel, bus travel, or hitchhiking. Unless she bought a car for cash. That was a possibility. But if she'd used the money to pay banks, as she'd told the 'recovery experts', she probably didn't have enough left to buy a car that would go very far.

For Le Cocq, every part of bounty hunting was gratifying, even the initial steps of setup. Finding available pieces to begin the puzzle that would eventually form a cohesive picture.

He would personally hit the bus terminals closest to her point of departure from the grid, but meanwhile, he'd get the spider working. That was what he called his extended network of eyes and ears. He'd have hundreds of people, including law enforcement, looking for someone who matched Clover Fields' description.

No. She hadn't done anything illegal, but cops needed deposits in their Paypal accounts as much as anybody else. They were good resources because they were out and about as opposed to desk bound or home bound, and looking around. Always looking. The same could be said of bike clubs. So he used them, too.

He spent a few days doing his research, setting his traps, catching up on his cable shows that he'd recorded, and doing laundry. By the time his network was fully activated, he was repacked and ready to go with a flight out of New Orleans.

CHAPTER ELEVEN

IT'S WHO YOU KNOW

Leon Russell – *Lady Blue*

"THIS IS GETTIN' to be a habit," Brash said when Raze called to say he needed another favor. He was teasing because Raze was the lowest maintenance friend he had.

"I know. I'd take the others back for this one. Believe me."

By the tone of Raze's voice, Brash could tell it was something more serious than car shopping.

"What do you need?"

"A face-to-face confidential. You. Me. And Brand."

"Brandon?"

Raze's eyes flitted toward stray girl. "Yeah. He in town?"

"Yeah. Where do you want to meet?"

"Here. First crew comes into the roadhouse at two tomorrow to get ready for opening at four. I got no deliveries scheduled. Nothin' goin' on. So we'd have the place to ourselves in the morning. I think that's safest."

"Safest?" There was a register of alarm in Brash's question.

"Yeah. Safest. Look. I know y'all are busy. I wouldn't be makin' this call if I had a choice."

"What time?"

"Twelve. I'll rustle up lunch."

"You don't hear back from me, it means we'll be there. If he's got somethin' he can't get out of, we'll make it work another way."

CLOVER WAS LISTENING to the call. When he put the phone down, she immediately said, "Who's Brand?"

"Brash's twin brother. He's got connections in your part of the world and might be able to help."

She was shaking her head. "This was a mistake."

"What was?"

"Bringing this to your door. These people... there's a reason why I left everything except what I could carry in that duffel and ran. These people are dangerous and they don't mess around."

Raze sat back. "You know the place where we took the Toyota?"

"Yes."

"That's the headquarters of the Sons of Sanctuary Motorcycle Club. They're real nice people when they're friends of yours. And they're straight arrow citizens when it works for 'em. But if the situation calls for it, they can also be the kind of people who don't mess around."

That news did not seem to calm her down. "All the *more* reason for me to leave you out of this! God! I don't want to be responsible for you or your friends getting hurt." With a look that resembled sincere trepidation, she said, "I'm not going to be the second woman to wreck your life."

What she said drove straight to the core of Raze Rouen and cracked the barrier that he'd so carefully erected. His features were soft, but his words were not. "Simmer down. There's no point in ratcheting up the drama."

"Drama." She looked at him like he was crazy. "It's not drama when you're talking about people with weapons and every intention to harm. Is that your version of 'calm down'? Didn't anybody ever tell you that one of the five things you should never do with a woman is tell her to calm down?"

Clover thought it was an odd time for Raze to suddenly grow a sense of humor and decide he was amused, and that served to stoke the fire that was causing her to fume. Visibly. He thought the fact that her nostrils were flaring was precious.

"Here's the thing. We're gettin' out ahead of things comin' to that. We're gonna take precautions to be sure that things *don't* come to that. You trust me with this?"

She searched his eyes for only a second before committing to an answer. "I don't think for a minute that that's the smart thing to do or the right thing to do. So I don't get why," she nodded, "but I do. Trust you, I mean." She paused. "But how are you going to 'get out ahead of this'?"

"I have a Plan A and a Plan B. If one don't work, the other will."

He made it clear that he was saying nothing more about it.

"You hungry?"

"Yes. For pizza."

"Pizza." Raze said it like he was talking about eating shit. He looked toward the refrigerator. "I might have a frozen one."

"Okay. I'll make it," she said, sounding as enthusiastic as if it was a treat and privilege.

They ate pizza in front of the TV while watching past episodes of "Comedians in Cars Getting Coffee". Raze wasn't completely sold on the conversation, but he did enjoy Seinfeld's cars.

Around one he said, "Well, I'd better get some clothes."

He started to get up from the couch, but Clover put

her hand on his forearm. He looked down at where her fair hand rested on the darkened weathered skin of his arm that was bare from having rolled up the sleeve of the Henley he wore. His eyes lifted to hers.

"Don't go," she almost whispered.

His eyes momentarily squinted in an expression that was akin to a wince. "You don't owe me that, stray girl. I'm not buying you."

"I know that, Raze. I'm not for sale. But I'm yours tonight. If you want."

His eyes drifted down to her full lips that looked dewy because of the lip gloss she'd applied after consuming half of a pepperoni, Italian sausage, mushroom, black olive, green pepper and parmesan pizza.

He thought he ought to just get his clothes and go to the studio. In stray girl's words, that would be the smart thing to do and the right thing to do. But he knew he wasn't going to do the smart thing or the right thing. He'd taken the punches life had given him. He'd be stupid to say no to the gifts.

When he opened his mouth, he said one of the least

romantic things he could say. "You got a condom?"

She blinked rapidly, pulled back, and a frown formed on her forehead. "No," in a tone with a duh implied. "When I thought about what I might need to run for my life, condoms did *not* come to mind."

He smirked, leaned closer, and dropped his voice. "Don't get hysterical."

She narrowed her eyes. "You've managed to hit two of the five things you should never say to a woman in one evening."

He had the nerve to smirk at that as well. "I might have one stashed in the office at the roadhouse."

"You might? Or you do?"

He raised an eyebrow at her tone. "You're mad about me havin' condoms over at the roadhouse?"

She huffed. "I'm not *mad* about it. Exactly. I just don't like the image of you with…"

He gaped. "You couldn't seriously be jealous that I have condoms at the roadhouse."

"I wouldn't go so far as to say jealous."

"No? What would you call it?"

"Unwanted thoughts."

"Unwanted thoughts," he repeated.

"Unwanted thoughts about you fucking people at your place of business."

"Fucking people," he repeated. She was too adorable to be for real.

"That's what you're saying, right? That you fuck people at the roadhouse."

He smiled in the most insufferable way possible. "Not every day."

"Ugh!"

"Are you serious? You're feelin' territorial about me after one kiss?" He said it like it was the stupidest thing he'd ever heard while belying the fact that he was open to the idea. Perhaps even feeling euphoric about her wanting to keep him for herself. And her outburst was reassuring him that she wasn't offering herself as some kind of misguided attempt to pay back a kindness.

"And a dance!" She said it with such authority, that he couldn't stop himself from chuckling.

As much as she longed to see that, the timing was

wrong. So she pushed his shoulder. "Do not laugh at me!"

"Alright. I won't laugh, but be honest. You did not believe I'm a novice with women."

He said it like a question and made it clear he was waiting for an answer.

She crossed her arms in front of her and pouted. "No." But the pout disappeared the second he leaned over to nuzzle her ear and whisper in it.

"Aside from everything else, like that I'm a man, I'm older than you."

She tilted her head back. "What, like three years?"

"Four." She rolled her eyes. "I'll be gone for five minutes. When I get back I'm going to show you the reasons why you're so glad I'm not a novice with women."

He heard her breath catch at that and smiled. The smiling thing was starting to become a habit. He scented her with a deep breath in. Like most things he did, she found that sexy enough to make her squirm uncomfortably.

Then he was gone.

He'd said five minutes. That meant she had enough time to change into something worthy of a lover like Raze Rouen. What would that be?

She'd just done laundry. Everything was clean, but that didn't mean that she had a trunk load of under-garments designed for seduction. She did, however, have a pretty set of red lacy lingerie.

Tearing into the bedroom she threw off clothes, lo-cated the bra and panties, then looked for something to put on over it. She had nothing sexy and was about to settle for her Sponge Bob night shirt, but on a whim she opened the door to Raze's closet. If he'd share his bed, he'd share his clothes. Right?

She pulled out a black ACDC concert tee. Perfect. And ran to the bathroom.

She let her hair down from the messy bun that had been in all day, the perfect hair for helmets, and tossed her hair a bit so it had that tousled look. She checked her makeup and heard him come back in just when she thought she was as ready as she'd ever be.

He was standing at the foot of the bed, but turned when she opened the bath door. Eyes darkening immediately as they scanned over her, he rasped, "Hey. I have a shirt just like that."

"Oh?" She looked down like she'd forgotten what she was wearing.

"Looks better on you though."

All of a sudden he felt like the very novice he'd assured her he wasn't. He held up three condoms like they were the Holy Grail.

"Ambitious?" She smiled sweetly. He answered with a small lopsided grin. "I like the way you think." When he didn't make a move from the spot where he stood, she held up her hands. "Welcome to your bedroom."

Cocking his head to the side, he drunk in the fact that she was anxious, and wanting to put her at ease was all the prompt he needed to have his usual self-confidence flood back into his body.

"Come here," he said in a voice slightly raspier than usual.

She hesitated, like she was trying to choose what she

wanted most. To assert herself by refusing to be bossed around. Or bring herself within striking distance of the guy who was starting to loom legendary from her perspective and find out what his hands felt like when given free roaming privileges.

She closed the distance between them wearing the flush that a woman wears when she's more than ready to be made love to.

He rested his fingertips lightly on the sides of her hips and gently pulled her body flush with his. "You nervous, stray girl?"

Her eyes cast down to his mouth and back up to his eyes. She licked her lips. "Maybe."

"What do I need to do to put you at ease?"

"Kiss me. Like you did before when…"

Raze decided he didn't need to wait for the end of that sentence. He got the gist. While he was plundering her mouth with the kind of kiss she would likely *never* forget, he was inching the concert tee up her body, the tips of his fingers keeping contact with her skin as they blazed a trail of first contact.

When he released her lips, he pulled the shirt the rest of the way up and off her body, which left her standing there as his fully embodied wet dream, wearing the red lingerie he'd fantasized about.

He stared for so long she began to feel self-conscious and brought her arms up to her chest. He caught her wrists and pulled her arms out.

"No. Don't hide. Let me enjoy."

For once, he managed to say the right thing. All she needed to know was that he liked what he saw.

She stepped forward and pushed his Henley up. He didn't waste time, but pulled the shirt over his head in one clean movement. She pressed a kiss between his pectoral muscles while he unfastened her bra.

"Are you going to take off your boots?"

He grinned. "Is it my bare feet you're after?"

"Not exactly."

Growling as he nuzzled her neck, he said, "What is it you're so eager to see? Hmmm?"

"Well…"

"If you can't say it, you can't see it. Come on," he

coaxed. "I want to hear it straight from those lips." He cupped her breast in a big hand that was a little calloused from the handlebars of his Harley.

"You want me to talk dirty?" She lifted her chin. "Alright, fucker. Show me your cock."

He chuckled. "You want a show? Get on the bed."

She pulled down the quilt and top sheet, scooted up so that her back was against the headboard and pulled her knees up under her chin. Once in place she watched as he stripped out of every stitch he was wearing, revealing a body made fit by healthy food, daily runs, and a set of free weights in the garage. He was proud of it and had every right to be.

When his cock sprang free and bobbed enticingly, she couldn't stay where she was a second longer. She walked on her knees to the edge of the mattress so she could reach out and wrap her fingers around his velvet-covered, swollen length. When she squeezed, his eyes glinted in the dim light of the room and he growled. "Harder."

She complied, watching his face as she experimented with different grips and levels of pressure.

Forcing her back on the bed he laved the nipple of one of her breasts with his skilled tongue until she was panting and writhing.

"Get the condom," she said.

He let her nipple go and smiled wickedly. "I don't think we're ready to go there."

"We are! We are!"

"I'll say when we are."

She roared her own version of a growl, but got very quiet when he pulled her panties free and teased her sex with light airy touches all around her nub, circling but not touching. She tried moving her body to force contact but he was good at evasion.

"Ruin. You're the Devil."

He shook his head. "Nah. I'm just the guy who's gonna show you why you want to stick around here."

That made her stop dead still. "You want me to stick around?"

"One thing at a time, stray girl. I'm tryin' to make love to you. Pay attention."

She grinned. "Yeah. I'm on board with that plan. Hence, the sweating, squirming, begging, and pleading."

He chuckled and grazed her clit as he slipped his third finger into her opening, which caused her to gasp. "Stop being cute and come for me."

"I'm not being cute! I'm being needy. There's a difference. And I'm not a trained whore with tricks like come on demand!"

"Okay." He was amused by her defensive outburst and the way it was delivered while panting for him. But at the same time, he was determined to give her the orgasm of her life. He added his ring finger to the massaging of her inner walls while rhythmically stroking her swollen button with his thumb. In less than a minute she'd exploded in a spectacular orgasm that left him hoping he'd never forget the sounds she made or the look on her face. But he wasn't too concerned with remembering. He was more concerned with earning an opportunity to recreate that look again and again and again.

She was clinging to him, nails dug into his shoulders, when he pulled away suddenly. Opening her eyes, she tried to get her brain to function well enough to perceive what was going on.

He was ripping open the condom package with his teeth and rolling it on to the most mind-blowingly perfect organ imaginable. She found the process fascinating and erotic, perhaps the most erotic thing she'd ever seen.

"That was soooooo sexy," she purred.

"What? Putting this condom on?"

"Don't play like you don't know." His sardonic smile coupled with hooded eyes gone dark and heated was her undoing. When he aligned himself at her entrance, she repositioned herself to accommodate. "Hurry up. Stop teasing."

He laughed. "You're awful greedy, stray girl."

"Just shut up and give me what I want."

He slid in slowly, allowing her body to adjust to his unusual size, never taking his eyes away from her face. He wanted to savor every second because intimacy with a woman like stray girl didn't come along every week.

Maybe not even in every lifetime.

"This what you want?" he asked.

She made a strangled noise that he took as a yes as she accepted him in his entirety.

Raze hadn't lied when he'd bragged that she'd be glad he wasn't a novice. He made love slowly and unselfishly, with purpose and stamina. By the time all three condoms were used, she was as limp as a rag doll and sleeping so soundly that she was snoring softly. Which, like so many other things about her, he found adorable.

He pulled the covers over them and spooned her from behind, acknowledging that he hadn't slept with a woman since the time he was a married man. Raze had been certain he'd never allow those kinds of feelings to be tapped again. But stray girl was, well, different. She brought out things in him that he'd never felt before, not even with his ex-wife.

Things like a longing that couldn't be quenched. A desire to be even closer when that was physically impossible. And, above all, a need to protect her from whatever might be coming.

He didn't know how it was possible for him to have such strong feelings in such a short time. But it was an undeniable fact and nothing was going to hurt stray girl so long as he lived and breathed.

SHE WAS ASLEEP when he eased out of bed. So he left a note on the pillow.

> *Gone for a run with Bless and set the alarm. So don't open the door. Back soon.*

She was still asleep when he got back. So he got in the shower, put on clean clothes and was leaving to open up the roadhouse kitchen and make sandwiches for the Fornight boys when she roused.

"Hey," she said, sounding sleepy.

He sat on the side of the bed and pushed hair back from her face. "Hey. I'm heading over for the meeting. I'm gonna set the alarm. Don't open the door. If you need something, call me. Or text me." He looked around. "Where's your phone?"

She pointed to her purse. He handed her the purse so she could pull out her phone.

"This is a burner."

"I know."

It looked small in his hand as he stared at it.

He sighed. "That was smart. Who'd you give this number to?"

"Henry Boyd."

"That's it?"

"That's it."

He nodded. "I'm putting my number in contacts."

"Okay."

"Back in an hour or so." He got up to leave.

"Raze?"

"Yeah?"

"Last night was amazing."

He gave her a boyish lopsided grin and a little shake of the head. "Yeah. Want more of that. Which means I need to make sure this thing followin' you around gets taken care of."

RAZE MADE SLICED chicken breast sandwiches on artisan bread and served them with thick cut potato chips and his best craft beer.

"Thanks for comin'."

"Doesn't need to be said." Brand assured him.

"It does," Raze argued. "I might be testin' the limits of my friendship with your brother." Brash scoffed and crossed his arms over his waist. "Don't judge till you've heard what I got to say."

"Then spill it," Brash said.

"My friend I got the car for?"

"Your friend?" Brash's eyes sparkled as he turned to his brother. "He means his woman."

Brand nodded and took a bite of sandwich. "This is good. Like the Dijon and the mushrooms. Nice pairing and gives it a little kick."

"Thanks. It's one of my own creations," Raze answered.

"If you two girls are done exchangin' recipes...?" Brash interjected. "You were sayin' something about your girl."

"She's in trouble."

"Think we got that, Raze. We're not the people folks call when they want to put together a bake sale." He looked at Brand. "Well, maybe he is."

Brand snorted good-naturedly, but said nothing.

"She stole money from the mob."

The Fornight brothers stopped chewing at the same time and donned identical expressions of amazed reaction to the short, but shocking sentence just blurted into the lunch conversation.

After a few beats Brash said, "Either I did not hear you right or this is a joke."

"Well, technically she didn't steal it. Exactly. But that's the case they're making."

He recounted Clover's story from the bag in her gym locker to the night she arrived at the roadhouse courtesy of Henry Boyd and a car that wouldn't start.

"Quite a story," Brash said and looked over at his brother, who spread out his hands as if that was a silent code between the two of them, and shook his head.

"I care about her," Raze said quietly.

"I think we got that, too," Brash said. "So what are you askin' us to do?"

Raze looked at Brand. "You got connections up there?"

"You mean New Jersey?"

"Yeah. That's what I mean."

Brand smiled. "Germane has connections every-where."

Raze glanced at Brash who nodded as if to confirm that what his brother said was true.

"I want to pay 'em off. Make sure the debt is settled and it's done and over with. For good," Raze said. "I guess what I'm sayin' is I don't know the best way to go about negotiating this."

Brash was familiar enough with Raze's finances to know that he was good for it.

Brand nodded approvingly and sat back. "These things are not usually personal. If you have the money, it's just a matter of pay off."

"Yeah." Raze nodded. "I figured as much."

"You got their contact info?"

"No. They were gonna come back to her in three days. Said they'd either take the money or her. She ran."

Brand looked at Brash. "So I need to put out the word to find out who's looking for her. When I find out, I'll go to the top. Make the deal." He looked at Raze. "They're going to want cash. It's just how they like it. I can get somebody in my New York office to give it to them. Then you pay me back. That work for you?"

Raze hadn't been friends with Brandon growing up because they hadn't even known Brand existed. But he looked so much like Brash and sounded so much like Brash, it was hard to not transfer those same feelings to Brash's twin brother.

Raze smiled. "I would be very grateful for that."

"She stickin' around after it's done?" Brash asked.

Shrugging, Raze said, "We haven't had that conversation specifically, but that plan has got my vote."

The Fornight brothers stood to go.

"Everybody's lookin' forward to free stuff on Bike Night. Day after tomorrow, right? Oh. Got a new guy from SoCal and he's a lady killer. Better lock your girl up 'cause he'll be comin' with us."

"Nah. She knows she has it good." Raze smiled.

Brash and Brand chuckled and said their goodbyes.

Raze walked back over to the house. As he was turning off the security system, he was calling out, "Just me."

Within seconds, she was in the kitchen. "How'd it go? What happened?"

"It's gonna be taken care of. I told you. I have friends who are good at gettin' things done."

She frowned. "What do you mean when you say 'taken care of'? These people... They're not going to just forget about it because you say they should."

He chuckled. "You say the damnedest things. That coffee still hot?"

"Tell me what's going on, Ruin! And, no, the coffee's not hot. You've been gone a long time. I turned it off forever ago."

"If you could wave a wand and solve this problem the easiest way possible, what would that be?"

She threw her hands up in exasperation and plopped into a chair. "Put a giant pile of cash in a bag and hand it to them. With a five percent tip for their inconvenience."

"Bingo. So that's what we're gonna do."

She stared, blank-faced and blinking. "What?"

"You heard me." He shuffled over to the cabinet to make a fresh coffee. "Your shift starts in two hours. We close at midnight on Tuesdays."

"You're making me nuts and you know it. How are you going to just hand them a bag of cash? I DON'T HAVE THE MONEY! IT'S GONE!"

Raze leaned back against the kitchen counter. "Simmer down. I told you everything's okay. You don't have the money, but I do. I've done alright."

Clover's lips parted to match the astonishment on her face. He could read a hundred thoughts flit through her mind and every one showed on her very expressive face.

"You're saying you're paying the debt. For me."

"That's what I'm sayin'."

She would have loved to have the luxury of thanking him for the offer, but declining. But she knew that would be even dumber than taking the money and paying off her creditors with it. The first time she realized she hadn't been breathing was when her lungs involuntarily gasped like a bellows, filling up and sending oxygen through her bloodstream.

"I just don't even know what to say." Her voice was almost a whisper.

"Just say thanks." He said it like it was no bigger favor than bringing her a slushee from Sonic.

She nodded. "Thanks." Her eyes wandered around the room. "It was going to take me half my life to pay off that money. I mean before the bag showed up in my locker. I'll still pay it back. I guess I'll just make payments to you instead of the bank. Or banks."

He smiled. "Sure. If you want."

A look of mild alarm crossed her face. "How are your friends going to find the right people? I don't even have names."

"Got it covered."

"How do you know? What if your friends give money to the wrong people? Then you're out your money and I've still got bad men coming to get me."

He chuckled as he walked over and pulled her to her feet. "Time for worryin' is over. You can relax now. Start thinkin' about the rest of your life." He leaned down, gently kissed her lips, then tugged lightly on her bottom lip with his teeth. "What you're gonna do." He kissed her a little longer, his tongue invading her mouth and pressing hers into an insistent tangle. "Who you're gonna do it with," he breathed into her ear, sending shivers up and down her body.

"Do it with," she repeated like she'd lost her mind, which could be partially true. Raze's kisses were like a gateway drug that led to wanting something stronger and more potent. "How long did you say until my shift?"

"An hour and forty-five minutes. I've only got an hour. You got some ideas about how I could spend that time?" He reached for her as he asked the question. She took a step forward to show that she was receptive to the idea of afternoon delight. Their faces were inches apart when he looked down and said, "This doesn't have anythin' to do with that."

It was a remark constructed in a way that could be open to wide-ranging interpretation. But she knew exactly what he meant by it.

"Hmmm," she said.

"What's that mean?"

"It means this has *something* to do with that."

"You don't owe me…"

"I don't owe you sex. Or feelings. Or anything except the money. Which I will pay back. Eventually. But knowing that you did this for me… I'm only human. You've taken care of me since I walked into the roadhouse. You even gave up your own bed because I was anxious about the studio. You took care of the car thing."

"I'm not a hero, stray girl. I did those things because you're so damn cute." He nuzzled her neck and inhaled the scent of green apple shampoo in her hair.

"Maybe so, but the point is, you didn't do it for sexual favors." When he didn't say anything, she added, "Did you?"

He chuckled. "Not consciously, but I'm bettin' there was a part of me that was hopin' you were gonna be in my bed *with* me."

"Would you still have done those things if you knew for sure there was no nookie to be had?"

He pursed his lips. "Yeah. I guess so."

"Well, there you have it then."

"There I have what?"

"My respect. My interest."

"Your body?"

She laughed. "All yours."

"Well, shut up and come here then," he said.

THE NEXT TWO days were sweet and easy. Raze was getting used to having a two-legged girl in his house. From time to time he thought it was downright scary how effortless it had been to fall into the comfort of sharing a house and a bed with Clover. Employees and people in town had taken to ribbing him about the change in his demeanor.

He didn't care.

His life had turned a corner when he got Bless. That dog gave him a reason to think that life wasn't just for shit. Then Brash demanded that he name something he wanted from life.

He had.

And for a long time he'd been satisfied with that. He had purpose. He liked that there was a reason to get up every day and, though some might laugh at the notion, he thought he served the community in his own way. He provided a place to loosen up. Have a drink or two. Eat some good food. Listen to music. Maybe laugh with friends. Maybe have a dance.

His roadhouse was all about fun, but running it was a serious business and he took it seriously. He supposed he deserved the reputation of being a purpose with a permafrown.

He'd expected that very little about his life would change until it was time to either move to assisted living or run the bike head on into a tree. The last thing he'd seen in his future was stray girl. But thinking back to the night she came through the door, he should have realized the hitch in his gut meant that fate had something extraordinary stumbling into his path.

It was too soon to call it a second chance at happiness, but the fact that he was feeling happy was undeniable. People could razz him all they wanted. The thing he was feeling, though he wasn't feeling compelled to give it a name, was worth it.

CHAPTER TWELVE

BIKE NIGHT

Steppenwolf – *Born to be Wild*

O F COURSE ANYBODY who wasn't bringing trouble was welcome at the roadhouse on Bike Night, but it was understood that bikers were *especially* welcome. Roadhouse and ice house owners loved them because they weren't committed to cocooning. Sometimes they left their houses at night, headed out for some open road, some live music, a juicy steak, cold beer, and good company. They lived a code based on the belief that life wasn't all about what's on cable or satellite or Youtube.

The band that called themselves Thunder showed up at five to set up so they'd be ready to start at six. When it came to pleasing bikers, classic rock was the way to go and nobody was better at recreating the songs they loved than Thunder. Raze had a decent sound system in the roadhouse, but Thunder wasn't the sort of band to take chances. They brought their own. Just in case. They told Raze one time that, "Professional musicians always have a Plan B. It's in our best interest to use our own equipment."

He'd told them that seemed like, "Sound wisdom. Might be applied to pretty much everything in life."

Julio and Carl were rolling the glass-topped ice case out to the end of the bar area. It made a tighter squeeze, but on nice evenings Bike Night included an option for customers to choose and grill their own steaks.

Bikers loved it. And so did Raze. Steaks grilling over mesquite-laced coals would make mouths water for a mile around. People driving by would follow their noses like canines. Those who liked heavy rock music would stay and eat. Those who didn't would never get out of their cars. Raze scored that as a double win.

The South Austin Meat Market delivered prime cuts. Raze ordered extra because he knew the SSMC was showing up in full force.

Julio's cousin always came to work as grill master. It was a job that required a certain kind of personality, part cook and part enforcer. Not just anybody was willing to correct a burly biker on grill technique or, when necessary, send him on his way. He pulled the big commercial barbeque outside using a trailer hitch and fired it up with a "secret" mix of charcoal and mesquite chips that had been soaked in water overnight.

Raze was on his way outside to make sure all the lightbulbs strung over the picnic area were working when he saw the sheriff coming his way.

"Raze." The sheriff stuck out his hand.

"John." Raze shook hands. He'd gone to high school with John McIlvaney, but was three years younger. He was junior varsity on the football team when John was a senior, being named all state in their division. "You want a beer?"

The sheriff shook his head. "Cain't do it."

"Good to know local law enforcement is serious about bein' on duty sober."

"Nah. It's not that." The sheriff's palm immediately came up to slap the gut that was threatening to lap over his belt. "The wife is threatenin' to withhold sexual attentions if I continue growin' out over my boots." Raze chuckled. "Whatever happened to the days when women didn't care what a man looked like? Christ. I miss those times."

Raze nodded agreeably.

"Do not bother to commiserate," John continued. "I'll bet you could still fit into your rented prom tux."

Raze shrugged. "I might've filled out a little since then."

"Yeah?" He glanced around. "Wouldn't mind one of those thick T-bones you do, but I think Marsha's makin' some casserole kinda thing."

"You're welcome to stop in and eat supper anytime."

The sheriff nodded. "Well. Just came by 'cause I saw it's Bike Night."

"That's a fact."

"Just remindin' you about the good residents of the

new suburban sprawl just over that way." He pointed to the southeast. "Swear to Christ, Austin's gonna take us over someday."

"Seems likely."

"Space travel's becomin' more and more appealin' all the time."

Raze smiled. "Havin' a hard time picturin' you on the way to Mars, John."

The sheriff sighed. "Can't argue that. Thing is, though, when the atmosphere is just right and you got the bay doors open, music carries over there to the subdivision. Then the goddamned phone calls get goin'. Like we got nothin' better to do than listen to people object to good times."

"Already made a concession in that direction. Band quits at ten on Bike Night, John." It went without saying that Raze had agreed to cut the live music at ten on week nights, but on weekends, bands played from nine to one. Full stop.

"I know. And it's appreciated. Just sayin' we're gonna be gettin' calls."

"I was here first."

"That's a fact."

Raze took in a deep breath and let it out. "You runnin' for re-election, John?"

"Believe I will."

"Well, you know I've been an admirer of the way you carry the office in the past. Count on my support."

John's face spread into a big smile. "Nice of you to wish me luck, Raze. I appreciate that." His face grew serious once again. "But I might not be runnin' unopposed like last time."

Raze narrowed his eyes. "Well, we definitely want to make sure you keep the job."

"That's what I wanted to hear. Y'all stay outta trouble tonight."

"Always."

"Yep."

The sheriff took long and surprisingly graceful strides to his marked SUV, the movement suggesting that he'd once been an athlete. Raze gave himself a moment of self-congratulations that he took reasonably good care of his body. He wouldn't wish military life on his worst enemy, but he had to admit that he had got some worthwhile things out of the experience. One of those things was a sense of pride in taking care of things.

"Startin' to smell temptin', Paco," Raze said to Julio's cousin on the way back inside.

"Just like you like it, boss." Paco grinned.

Raze headed for the house to take a shower and change clothes before customers started arriving.

After giving Bless a ten second pet, Raze hollered, "Hello!"

Clover appeared at the kitchen door almost instantly with a welcome look in her eyes, the kind he could get used to. She'd been watching TV but she was dressed for work and he was not happy with what he saw. Even though it made him hungry, thirsty, and every other kind of needy.

"Go change your clothes," he said gruffly.

He saw a second of hurt in her eyes just before her smile fell. She had the most expressive face he'd ever seen. Every thought was right there on display and readable as a neon sign. She looked down at the jeans and tee shirt.

Raze didn't have the servers wear roadhouse uniforms. He had them wear classic rock concert tees which he collected from Ebay for that purpose. She'd picked out a faded blue Thin Lizzy shirt from the Bad Reputation tour, Dublin, 1977. It made her eyes pop like they were supernatural. It clung lovingly to her curves like it had been made for her body.

"What's wrong with this? I thought it looked good."

"It does. That's the problem."

It took another couple of seconds for her to catch on that he was paying her a backhanded compliment. When she got it, she laughed. "You feeling territorial? About me?" She closed the distance between them and put her arms around his neck.

"Not at all. I'm concerned as your boss. I want to spend my time makin' sure people have a good time and use their credit cards. I do not want them havin' a good time trying to touch this." He took her arms from around his neck and pulled her into the bedroom. "What other shirts did you pull outta the pile?"

She huffed, but picked up the White Snake from the Slip of the Tongue tour 1990.

"No," he said. "Too suggestive."

"Too suggestive," she snickered. "Are you a bike-riding roadhouse owner or are you my great-aunt?"

"Funny. What else you got?"

She pulled the next shirt from the pile. Also Whitesnake from the Lovehunter tour 1980. It depicted a naked woman riding a snake.

Raze jerked it out of her hand. "You are *not* wearin' this! EVER!"

"Raze! It was in the stack of shirts you told me to pick from."

"Did you look at these?"

She narrowed her eyes. "Didn't you buy these?"

He hesitated. "I didn't buy these for you."

She laughed. "Who'd you buy them for?"

"Somebody who's not you."

"Oh. Well, then." She held up the Slip of the Tongue

shirt. "I don't like the idea of a man telling me how to dress, but since you get to pick what *everybody* wears... this or this?"

He growled softly. "I'm takin' a shower."

"Okay." She smiled brightly.

"I'm tellin' Dunk to keep an eye on you tonight."

"Sure." She nodded. "But my spilling beer on crotches method works even better than scary looking bald guys."

His mouth twitched in spite of himself. "Tomorrow I'm shoppin' for new shirts."

"Go take your shower."

RAZE CAME OUT of the shower with a towel around his waist, looking lollipop good. Before he could get into his clothes, Clover planted her face in his chest and inhaled the intoxicating goodness of soap and fresh clean man. What started out as an innocent I'm-heading-to-work kiss soon had tongue and lips heading south toward Raze's enticing happy trail and eventually ended up as a blowjob that made him see stars, right before his knees threatened to buckle.

He told himself that no man alive could say no to Clover's beautiful rose-colored mouth and magical tongue. Even the owner of a roadhouse, late for work and expecting a big night, couldn't be expected to turn that down. He'd have to be inhuman.

HE JUMPED INTO clothes, pushed his fingers through his hair, and gave Clover a heart-stopping grin.

"Wait. You forgot your phone," she said as they were closing the kitchen door. She noticed it was on the counter.

"I don't take it to work. If it rings, I can't hear it. And I don't like that vibrate thing."

She chuckled. "Sensitive. I like that."

His eyes drifted over her again. "You better always have a pitcher of beer at the ready."

"I will." She raised her chin and smiled impishly.

THIBAUT LE COCQ mused that he really didn't deserve to be so lucky, but he'd take it anyway.

He was set to fly out of New Orleans in three hours when he got a call from Lock Manatee, the Stars and Bars' president. The SBMC was headquartered in Picayune Mississippi, just two and a half hours from Lafayette. Close enough to be considered Le Cocq's home territory. He liked working with SBMC because they were completely without scruples. They were one of the contacts who got his message, that he was looking for a girl named Clover Fields, not an a.k.a. Included was a description of height, weight, age, and her student ID photo from Columbia wasn't bad.

One of the SBMC members had been passing through south central Texas. He wasn't wearing colors. After what had happened in Waco, the members of the Stars and Bars MC who were not incarcerated were not welcome in the Lone Star state.

He was about to get a cheap room for the night when he saw the lights of the roadhouse and stopped in on impulse. The man wasn't looking for Clover Fields, but there was a girl waiting tables who'd drawn attention to herself by soaking a guy's crotch with a pitcher of beer. He thought there was something familiar about her, but couldn't place it. So he forgot all about it until the next day as he was roaring east on I10 lost in thoughts both shallow and ambitious. All of a sudden, he remembered the 'flier' from Le Cocq and pulled over to call the SBMC president, Lock Manatee.

"If it's her, we'll be lookin' for our cut," Lock said.

"If it's her," Le Cocq replied smoothly, "I'll be payin' your cut and I might also be lookin' for a place to stash the merchandise."

"For how long?"

"Couple days tops."

"Might be open to that. We'll give you a nice fat discount for repeat business."

Le Cocq chuffed at that, knowing he'd be gouged. "Just what I'd expect."

He ended the call and started throwing things in a bag, liking that he'd be able to take his own vehicle. He had a custom van outfitted for the very purpose of transporting human cargo who did not want to be transported. It was designed to make things easy on himself, but unfortunately he didn't get to use it nearly often enough. Jobs didn't normally land right in his backyard. Or close enough.

He pressed the code into the keypad that disarmed the separate security system on his four-door garage.

The van was white. Not the color you'd choose if you wanted to attract attention, which made it perfect. White was good because it was so common. People look right past white vans and never suspect they might be carrying anything more questionable than flowers or auto parts.

As he was driving away he started an audio book on gardening. He wasn't home enough to tend to tomatoes, cucumbers, and squash, but he thought someday he might be. So he reasoned that he might as well spend the drive time productively.

After driving through the night he reached the Austin city limits as the sun was coming up. He checked into a chain motel and put the Do Not Disturb sign on the door so he could get some sleep.

CHAPTER THIRTEEN

BAD REPUTATION

Boz Scaggs – *Look What You've Done To Me*

J UST AS RAZE had feared, customers looked at stray
girl like they wanted to drag her out back and eat
her alive. That damn Bad Reputation shirt made her
look like an angel. Or maybe it was that she looked so
happy. The image of her coming in out of the rain, just
a few days before, looking lost and maybe scared flashed
across his mind. That was followed by the flush of male
pride that filled his chest, knowing he was the one that
had put that look on her face.

The roadhouse had never been so packed. Never.

The combination of Thunder's growing popularity
and the fact that he'd invited the entire SSMC made it
hard for the servers to get to the tables, even with the

bay doors open and half the crowd spilled outside.

He stayed behind the bar most of the night. Luke and Carl needed the help. It was an all-hands-on-deck kind of night if ever there was one.

ALL NIGHT LONG, whenever Clover looked toward the bar, she knew Raze would look her way within seconds and get that twinkle. It wasn't quite a smile, just a *you're mine* sort of proprietary assurance. She'd never been claimed. Never even. come close to being claimed. At least not in the way of a man taking hold and saying, "Mine," with an indisputable manner.

If she'd been asked how she might feel about that a week earlier, she would have said she wasn't interested. Yet there she was in a Texas roadhouse almost preening in response to Raze's possessive gaze.

She decided that everything depended on who wanted to own you. And why.

About midway through her shift, she headed past the end of the bar with an empty tray. Raze lifted the tray from her shoulder, set it on the end of the bar, turned her toward the dance floor and guided her there with his hand at the small of her back.

As he took her in his arms, he leaned down and rumbled softly in her ear, "Dance with me."

In response she grinned shyly, while suppressing a public display of shivers as a result of the thrill she got from Raze's breath on her ear.

The band didn't play many slow numbers, but once an hour or so they slowed things down to give couples some up close time. Raze hadn't been waiting for the right moment. It was purely impulsive, but the fact that it wasn't planned didn't make it feel any less right.

As she molded into his body, he marveled at how it felt like she was made to be there. He turned his head to scent her hair, thinking how curious it was that he'd never known he loved the aroma of green apples. He knew that grabbing one of the key personnel on what could easily be the busiest night of the year wasn't a good business decision. But no healthy bottom line could ever feel as good as the woman pressed so close to his belt buckle.

While they danced close, he said, "Got word that your situation is taken care of. No more worries." He leaned back to look at her face. "Yeah?"

He saw the gratitude in her eyes when she nodded, but he knew there was more there than just thanks. She was feeling the thing happening between them just as he was. He was sure of it.

She gave him the kind of little squeeze that was more affection than seduction and his heart gave way a little more.

When the song ended they both felt pangs of regret, but silently agreed that the duty calling didn't mean they wouldn't pick up where the song left off later. At home.

Clover continued the circuit. Rushing here and there to make sure everybody was covered. Weaving in between tables and around clusters of people to deliver drinks and food with a smile that felt more genuine than it ever had before in her life. It struck her that she might not have known what happiness felt like, just that it was possible. It also struck her how odd it was to find someone as miraculous as Raze under such peculiar circumstances. Life was strange.

After checking on her section just after nine, she started back toward the bar and almost faltered a step. She didn't see Raze at the bar. Instead her eyes landed on a guy sitting alone on a stool at the end staring at her.

In a hundred years she couldn't have described why it felt different from the looks she'd gotten from a hundred other customers. It just did. It was unsettling. Disturbing. Predatory.

Certainly there was nothing sinister about his looks. He had regular, even pleasant features. He was wearing jeans, boots, a collared polo shirt, and a baseball cap. The alarm had nothing to do with his looks and everything to do with his look.

She looked away quickly, knowing that her facial expressions betrayed her anytime she wasn't working at hiding her thoughts. She carried her tray back to the kitchen. And walked out the back door.

RAZE HAD BEEN outside chatting with some of the members of the SSMC, getting to know new members and meeting wives for the first time. He was feeling good. After all, it was exactly what he'd wanted. A whole bunch of people having a really good time. He couldn't imagine what more a person could want from life. Unless it was stray girl.

He'd kept trying to keep thoughts like that from taking root. He was too old to be guided by impulse and he'd only known her for a few days. Still, he didn't think he'd ever had the kind of connection, and peace, with anybody that he had with Clover. Spooning with her in the early morning hours, he'd gotten overly sentimental about how good it felt, how he would have liked to freeze the moment in time. Listening to her deep breaths. Feeling her silky smooth skin. Smelling that girly green apple shampoo that she liked.

Brandon Fornight pulled him aside. "Arrangements have been made for payment. By tomorrow morning it will be done and over with."

Raze breathed a big sigh of relief. "This is one that's

gonna be hard to repay."

Brand grinned. "You're wrong about that. Best steak I've ever had. I'm going to hire that guy." He looked toward Paco. "He elbowed me out of the way, said I didn't know what I was doing, and seven minutes later gave me back a steak I'll be dreaming about for a long time."

"I got the money," Raze said.

"I know. I'm not worried about it."

Raze nodded. "Have a good time. And, you know, thank you."

It was about nine thirty when he stepped back inside.

Marjorie confronted him. "Where'd that new girl go? Her section's bordering on mob violence."

Raze scowled as his eyes scanned for Clover. Nothing. "How long's she been gone?"

"How am I supposed to know that? It's kinda busy, ya know."

He checked the kitchen and the ladies' restroom, all the while telling himself to stay calm. But as he jogged toward the house, he realized something was out of place. That was the first twinge of full-blown panic. The Jeep was gone.

The Jeep was gone.

The Jeep was gone.

The back door was unlocked. The big rolling bag she'd brought with her was still there, but some of her clothes were gone. Like she'd grabbed what she could carry in her hands and run.

Hurrying back to the kitchen his eyes fell on something else out of place. Her driver's license. It was sitting on the table alone, conspicuously face up, and angled so as to be easily spotted.

Something had scared her enough to make her run out in the middle of Bike Night. No time to write a note or say goodbye, but she left the license as a message or a clue that he had no idea how to interpret.

Raze realized he was breathing heavy. His heart was racing too.

He ran around the building to the front of the road-house where the bikes were parked. Most of the SSMC had called it a night. A few remained including Brash, who was already on his bike with his woman when Raze called out to him, stopping him from turning the engine over.

Brash sat straddling the bike and waited. "You look a little wild-eyed, brother," he said when Raze came close. Even in the dim light of the parking area he could see that something was wrong.

"She's gone."

"Who?" Brash's eyebrows knitted together as his eyes cast back and forth around the area. "Oh. The, um…"

Raze grabbed two fistfuls of leather cut. "I need help."

Brash put his hands on Raze's wrists and said, "I know. Turn loose so I can get off this machine." He looked at Brigid over his shoulder. "You catch a ride with Mom?"

"Sure. Of course." She nodded, throwing a concerned look toward Raze. "See you at home," she said to Brash.

"Raze," Brash said quietly. "You know you can't force a woman to stay if she has other plans."

Raze was shaking his head furiously. "No. It's not like that. She *ran*. We don't have time to waste making you believe me. She left her stuff. Left her driver's license on the kitchen table, like some kind of... I don't know, fucked-up message. Somethin' spooked her. Spooked her so bad she didn't feel like she could take the time to find me." His eyes were imploring Brash to hear his words and believe what he was saying. "She just *ran*."

Brash's eyebrows were still drawn together. "She left her stuff? And her license?"

Raze grabbed his hair with both hands. He'd been through more than his share of stuff, in the military and elsewhere. And he'd felt fear before, but not the way he was feeling fear at that moment.

"Doesn't make sense," Raze said. "Brand told me it was handled. Said the money was gonna find its way to the right place tomorrow mornin'. So I don't get it. Unless somebody was hunting for her and didn't get the message."

Brash gave a nod so small it was almost imperceptible. He looked around. Brand was gone. Pulling out his phone, he sent a text. If Brand was riding, he wouldn't get the message until he stopped. Probably.

"I gotta find her," Raze said. "I know I've been askin' a lot…"

"That's not a consideration and you know it," Brash said as he finished typing. "You got somebody who can shut down and close up?"

Raze looked back at the roadhouse like he'd completely forgotten he was a business owner. "Give me two minutes and meet me at the house."

Raze jogged inside and grabbed Luke. "You've been wantin' a chance to step up. Right?"

Luke looked over Raze's shoulder like he was trying to figure out what brought that on. "Right," he said simply.

"Well, this is it. I need you to close down tonight. You think you can handle that?"

"Think I can." The fact that Luke didn't hesitate

made Raze feel good about walking off. Not that he wouldn't have done it anyway.

"Call me when you're ready to engage the security system."

Luke nodded. "Alright. I will."

The band was packing up and the crowd had thinned to the usual week night numbers. Everybody knew their job, but Raze didn't care about any of that as he made his way to the house.

"What are you doin' out here?" he asked Brash. "Door's open."

"Door may be open, but your dog doesn't know you gave me permission to walk in."

Raze stepped in front of him, opened the screen door, and held it for Brash. He took a few seconds to reassure Bless that Brash was okay with him.

"See?" He pointed to Clover's license.

"Why would she leave this?" Brash asked. "Looks real deliberate."

"It does. And I don't know."

"Did she ever say anything about where she would

go if she was…? Well, when she came here in the first place she was headed somewhere. Right?"

"West. Maybe west Texas. Maybe New Mexico. I told her that, as smart as she'd been to lose her phone and stay away from what connected her to her former life, that if she ever got pulled over, they'd ask for her driver's license. Then she and her location would be in the system."

Brash looked somber as he waited for Raze to go on. "Then she asked me…" Raze straightened. "That could be it. She asked me where I'd go if I was her. Said I'd go to Cajun country. Lafayette Parish."

Bless growled softly. Raze thought she might still be unsettled by Brash's late night visit. So he shushed her. "Shhh, Bless. S'alright." He reached down to pet her, but she had her ears pricked toward nothing Raze could see and his attentions didn't seem to garner the usual interest. She remained focused on something only she could hear.

Raze grabbed the back of his own neck like he needed to hold himself together and looked up at Brash.

"Christ. There's lots of road between here and there. Any ideas?"

Brash shook his head. "Soon as Brand gets my message, he's gonna get involved. I'm thinkin' that maybe we should also give my pop a call. He's good at solving problems. Creative, you might say. And he's got resources even I don't know about."

Raze took in a deep sigh. "You know what I want to do is go get in my truck and start drivin'."

"That's your heart talkin'. I'm glad your head is winnin'. So far. 'Cause takin' off to run her down without knowin' for sure where she's goin'?" Brash shook his head again. "That'd be crazy. Needle in a haystack. There'll be other ways of dealin'. Just hang tight."

Without warning Bless sprang to all four feet with a terrifyingly loud snarl and hackles raised. It was so fast and so loud it startled both men.

THIBAUT LE COCQ ate his burger and fries, which weren't half bad, drank his beer, which was cold and local craft, and enjoyed the band while the overall sense of satisfaction he had from knowing the job was all but done settled around him like a second skin. Sooner or later the girl's shift would end. It'd be easy enough to grab her later, either in the parking lot or after following her home to whatever shithole she was hiding in.

He'd made eye contact with her earlier while she was scurrying about. She'd looked away quickly. He assumed that was because she misinterpreted his interest as sexual and maybe she wasn't the kind to be flattered by a stranger's stare.

When she was out of sight for half an hour, he didn't think much of it. He figured she was on her dinner and restroom break. When that half hour started to look more like an hour, he got that itch in his gut that told him something was amiss.

He slid off the barstool, laid a fifty dollar bill on the bar and walked toward the back. He checked both restrooms before heading to the kitchen.

James, Julio, and Marquita, another cousin of Julio's who helped on busy nights, looked up when Le Cocq entered through the swing doors. His eyes quickly scanned the room.

"Help you?" James said in his gruff way with an eyebrow raised.

"Sorry. Lookin' for the restroom," Le Cocq said.

Using a spatula, Julio pointed toward the door through which Le Cocq had just come. "Go back out that way. Go to the other side of the bar and turn left."

"Oh. Okay."

Marjorie almost ran him down as he stood there. The servers weren't expecting anybody to be stopped dead still just inside the kitchen, but especially not on a night that depended on everybody bringing their best hustle.

"What the…?" she said.

"Sorry," Le Cocq mumbled.

There was only one place left to check. The office. And the only place it could be was down the short hallway to his left.

He didn't expect to find Clover Fields there so the fact that she was nowhere to be seen didn't come as a big surprise. Likewise, it wasn't a big shock to find that there was a backdoor on the other side of the office.

"Fuck," he growled low in his throat.

He took his baseball cap off, ran his hand over his head, and put it back on facing the other way. Maybe she'd gotten sick and taken off. Or maybe she had her own version of gut instinct that was more or less reliable, as his was, and had hightailed it after that eye lock.

No one was around so he tried the back door to see where it went. The handle turned. If it had an automatic lock-on-close mechanism, that was okay. His business inside the roadhouse was concluded.

There was not much behind the building. An expanse of grass that was maybe twenty yards deep led to a wood siding house sitting all by itself with an eight-foot chain-link fence around the yard in back. There was what appeared to be a separate garage. No cars in sight, but there was a light on in the house.

He was just about to investigate when he heard voices headed his way so he plastered himself against the back wall of the roadhouse where he'd be in the cover of shadows.

From what he could make out of the conversation, two guys were concerned about a certain young lady's sudden departure. He waited until they were in the house and crept forward taking up a post on the side of the house where he could hear the conversation through the screen door.

He congratulated himself on getting lucky a second time with the run. He'd taken the first bit of luck for granted and let her get away. He wouldn't make that mistake a second time.

After hearing that they thought she was headed for Lafayette Parish, which just happened to be his own backyard, he could have left. But he stayed to learn that they had no plan other than to make a plan.

When he turned to jog toward the van in the parking lot on the other side of the roadhouse, he heard a hair-raising snarl that caused him to freeze temporarily. But within a fraction of a second his own flight impulse was firing on all cylinders. He abandoned the plan to sneak back to his van and sprinted the whole way there.

WHILE RAZE AND Brash were trying to figure out what had Bless acting so aggressive, she lunged and tore straight through the screen door. They both followed, running after her all the way to the parking lot, where they witnessed her chase a white van spewing gravel as it peeled onto the pavement. She chased it for an eighth of a mile, then jogged back and came straight to Raze, wagging her tail.

Raze looked at Brash. "What was that about?"

"How am I supposed to know?"

"You're supposed to know because you trained the dog for protection."

"I didn't *personally* train the dog. But Christ. I'll send somebody over to fix the screen door."

"Don't give a damn about the screen door right now. I want to find that stray…" He caught himself. Calling Clover 'stray girl' didn't feel like an endearment when he knew she was running, scared, driving a car with registration and insurance in his name, unable to produce any identification, much less a driver's license, with nothing but a few days' tips in her pocket. "Clover. I just wanna find her."

Brash felt his phone vibrate in his pocket. Glancing at the blue light of the screen in the darkness he could see that it was his brother. "Christ, finally. You stop for Dairy Queen on the way home."

"What...?"

"Never mind. We got a situation. I'm puttin' you on speaker. Raze is here." Brash held the phone between them and selected speaker. "You sure the thing's been handled? 'Cause somethin' happened tonight that caused our girl to go runnin' outta here not takin' anything with her but a change of clothes and the car Raze got her. She even left her driver's license as some kind of message."

"On it. Finding the kink in communications and then we'll get it sorted out."

"Quick like. Raze is feelin' understandably anxious. You gotta get in touch with whoever put a bounty on her and make sure every cockroach in the world knows it's been retrieved."

"You think that's what happened? Bounty hunter scared her into running?"

"It's the only thing that makes sense. At least to me. Bounty hunter or a wannabe. Depends on how far and wide they spread the word that there's treasure in her return. I'm callin' Pop to get his thoughts on the thing."

"Keep you posted."

"Yep."

Brash ended the call and scrubbed a hand over his face. "That coffee pot of yours work?"

On the walk back to the house, Brash dialed Brant. "Yeah. I know it's late. And you know I wouldn't call to shoot the shit." Pause. "We got a situation that could use your perspective."

By the time Brash, Raze, and Bless had walked back to the house, Brant was more or less up to speed.

"She's drivin' a fire-engine-red Jeep Liberty. Older model, but it don't shy away from attention. Car and insurance are in Raze's name." His eyes sliced toward the license still sitting on the table. "She's got no ID on her." Pause. "Right. Not even a driver's license. And we're not a hundred percent sure, but there's reason to believe she might be headed to Lafayette Parish." As he heard that recounted out loud, Raze was silently praying that she was driving well below the speed limit.

Brash lowered the phone so that the speaker end was a little away from his mouth as he turned to Raze. "What's she wearin'?"

Raze didn't have to give that too much thought because they'd had a semi-serious discussion about her attire for the evening.

"A Thin Lizzy shirt. Blue. Says 'Bad Reputation'." Raze blinked a couple of times. "Unless she changed. I guess that's possible, but there's no doubt she left in a big hurry."

"Did you get all that?" Brash asked Brant on the phone and then paused to hear his dad's reply. "Well, 'course she could pull over and change. He thinks she might've grabbed a few things. So we're not a hundred percent sure." Pause. "Come on, Pop." Pause. "I don't..." Pause. "You don't..." Pause. Brash sighed.

"Guess you're the boss."

When Brash sat down at the kitchen table, Bless immediately came over, put her head on his thigh, and began wagging her tail as she looked up into his eyes with great expectations of hands-on affection.

"So *now* you want to be friends?" he asked, even as he reached out to stroke her head.

Raze set a cup of coffee in front of Brash and sat down, noting that Brash was avoiding eye contact. "Spill it?"

"You know Pop. He's got his own ideas about things." Brash still wasn't looking at him.

"Yeah. I know him. What the hell does that mean?"

"He says that favors come in all kinds of varieties and sizes. He says that he'll put some feelers out, make a few calls, in honor of your friendship with me." Brash took a sip of coffee. "But he says you know how it works. The SSMC takes the protection of our women very seriously. As a matter of fact, you'd be right if you said it's top priority. He says, if you want the kind of balls to the wall full stop commitment that comes with being part of the SSMC, everybody feelin' your problem like you feel your problem? It's yours. But you have to be a member of the SSMC."

Raze took in a sharp breath then squinted his eyes. "That's how it works now? I thought y'all were more democratic."

"He says in this case a vote's not needed 'cause he *knows* you'd get a majority."

"Why would it matter to him? Not sure I get it."

"He said you belong in the SSMC. You've always belonged. And, these are his words, not mine. He said since you seem to be havin' trouble findin' your way to where you belong, he's gonna give you a little shove in the right direction."

"So your dad is not above shake down."

Brash laughed and shook his head. "No. He's got his own code. Mainly goes like this; whatever it takes to keep family and club members safe and happy."

The two men stared at each other for a full minute in silence before Raze gave a shrug and a simple, "Okay."

"You sure?" Brash said.

Raze leaned forward slightly. "Surprised you're askin' me that. 'Cause I know for a fact you got a woman."

It was enough said.

Raze wasn't bothered or resentful about Brant's tactics. In an odd way he was flattered. And Brant was right about the fact that, if Becky hadn't taken over Raze's life, he probably would've prospected at the same time as Brash.

Fucking Becky. The club had never come right out and said they didn't like her, but the feeling was communicated in non-verbal ways. Becky felt it too, which was undoubtedly why she hated the SSMC and didn't want Raze anywhere around them.

That was then. Now there were a hundred good reasons to be part of the club and, off the top of his head, he couldn't think of even one reason why not.

Brash punched Brant's contact. "He says okay." Pause. "Yeah. Alright."

"What'd he say?"

"He told me not to tell you what he said."

Raze gave him a look that said, "If you value your life, you will answer my question now."

"Alright. I'll tell you, but consider it a confidence. He said he's callin' every club between here and there. Three of our guys have taken some of the fast rides from Wrecks to try to catch up with her on I10. The rest have already lit out on bikes. Good news is that it's the middle of the night and fewer cars. Bad news is it's dark outside. If they don't catch her, they'll go on to Lafayette and meet up with the Cajun Devils, who're already preparing to lay down a grid network."

"Cajun Devils?"

"They're allies of the SSMC. They've been wanting us to come in with them on an interstate trucking company. This could give them the chance they need to show Pop they'd make good partners. They'll be callin' in markers and spendin' money around the parish where needed to turn over every rock."

"That's good." Raze nodded. "Why did he not want me to know that?"

"He wouldn't care if you knew that part. It was the other part he told me to keep to myself."

"The other part was?"

"That all of this was in the works before you said yes."

Raze nodded thoughtfully. "I can't just sit around here. I'm goin'."

"You sure that's the best move?"

"If she went straight to Lafayette, she'd be there around three. Best move. Bad move. Just don't factor. I can't sit around here."

Brash sighed. "Let's drop Bless off with Rescue. I'll go with you."

"Bless goes. I don't know how long we'll be gone."

Brash shrugged. "Up to you."

Raze turned to Bless. "Go squat."

Bless headed for the dog door obediently.

"You taught your dog to go on command?" Brash asked in a tone full of admiration.

"I did. Comes in handy." He grabbed Clover's driver's license and Bless's leash then looked around for his phone. But his hand hovered over the spot on the counter where he always left his phone.

"What is it?"

"It's not my phone," Raze said quietly. "It's her burner. She took my phone and left the burner. Took my charger, too."

"Why would she do that?"

"I couldn't call the burner. Don't know the number. But I could call my own phone and it wouldn't hurt her chance of gettin' away."

"Jesus. You got one of them."

"One of what?"

"A smart woman. Sorry, brother."

Raze had no patience for jokes. "Shut up and give me your phone."

Brash handed it over and Raze dialed his own number. It rang for a bit and then went to voicemail. So he left himself a message.

"It's me. I'm callin' from Brash's phone. Don't know why you're not answerin', but I'm leavin' a message just in case. Got a lot of friends out lookin' for you while we're tryin' to find out who didn't get the message your situation's been managed. Call me the instant you get this. I'm on the way. Won't say where. Just... what we talked about. Call me back on this number."

Raze handed the phone to Brash. "Turn up the volume. Keep it on find *and* vibrate."

Knowing how he'd feel in Raze's place, Brash chose to let his friend get away with taking on some alpha behavior that would not have been allowed to pass under other circumstances without a challenge. He nodded, took the phone, and slid it into his jeans pocket. No matter how loud the environment was, he'd feel the vibration if she called.

Raze's truck had a custom hydraulic lift so that he could transport his bike if he wanted to. They used it to load Brash's Harley, and headed east.

Both men were lost in their own thoughts. At length, Raze said, "Why didn't she just come get me if she was worried? God knows I wasn't far away."

"I can't pretend to know how women think. But if you're askin' for a guess, I'm goin' with that she didn't

269

want to bring any kind of trouble to your roadhouse. Wanted to keep you out of it. You and your business. Whatever it was that scared her, I'm thinkin' she might've wanted to lead it away from you. She was in a big hurry, but she tried to leave some clues that she wasn't going because she's got no feelings for you."

Brash reached for his phone when it vibrated. It was Brandon.

"Yeah?"

"Took some time to track down the decider at his estate. Took more time to convince his people to put him on the phone. Says he gave an exclusive on the contract to a guy he works with pretty often. Apparently he outsources the work because this guy never fails. He said it's possible that getting the word to him might have fallen through the cracks because rescinding a contract isn't something they've done before. Ever."

"So what now?"

"Now he's going to make sure the hunter gets the message. Or else."

"Or else what?"

"Or else he could end up with a bad reputation."

"Brother. Is that a genuine concern for the man?"

"Yeah. It's everything. Breaking a deal... If these people didn't think they could believe each other, their organizations would implode from within. Overnight."

"Hmmm."

"You want the bad news?"

Brash felt himself tense. He didn't react because he didn't want Raze to be alarmed, whatever it was. "Yeah," he said evenly.

"The bounty hunter is named Thibaut Le Cocq. And you're not going to believe where he lives."

At least a dozen expletives were trying to explode from Brash's mouth at maximum volume, but for Raze's sake, he kept the lid on.

"Okay. We're on the road headed toward Lafayette. Keep us posted."

RAZE WAS DRIVING, trying not to think about what could happen to Clover if the bounty hunter found her first. He happened to glance at the clock and felt a little shock run through his system. It was twelve thirty. He'd completely forgotten about the roadhouse, which had been his entire life just a few days ago.

"Luke was supposed to call when he was ready for me to come set the alarm," he told Brash. "I need to use your phone."

It shook him that he'd forgotten about what was going on at the roadhouse. He'd come to terms with the fact that he wanted stray girl for more than a pass-through thing. But he hadn't thought in terms of having fallen for her.

In a week's time.

He wasn't sure he thought it was possible to love somebody, really love them, in such a short time, but if that's what fate had given him, he wasn't backing away from it.

Luke's cell number was in the phone that Clover had with her. So Raze called the roadhouse land line. There was a phone in the office and an extension in the bar that didn't ring, but did light up. Everything depended on Luke being where he could see it.

"Roadhouse," Luke answered after three rings.

"Luke," Raze said.

"Tried to call, boss."

"Yeah. Lost my phone. So listen up."

Two years before, he'd run the same background check on Luke that he ran on everybody interviewing who'd be handling cash and credit cards. Looked clean, but giving over the security codes was a whole other universe. He'd never given the code to anybody. And yet he didn't hesitate to tell Luke where to find a spare key in the office, what the code was, and walk him through how to set the alarm.

As he was giving away the keys to the kingdom, he was thinking he'd gladly have all the money and hard work go up in smoke to get stray girl back unharmed.

"If I'm not back tomorrow when it's time to set up, you know how to do it?" Pause. "Okay, then. I guess you just got yourself a promotion to manager." Pause. "If something comes up, call this number."

"This is a land line. I don't know the number you're callin' from."

"Right." Raze handed the phone to Brash. "He needs to write down your cell number."

Brash gave Luke his number and ended the call.

THIBAUT LE COCQ had something in common with the SSMC. He, too, was spreading the word that he was looking for someone who fit Clover Fields' description. Someone who was probably wearing a blue Thin Lizzy tee that read Bad Reputation.

He let the Stars and Bars know that, if they intercepted her before he did, he'd split the bounty with them. Right down the middle. Fifty fifty. Since they weren't previously engaged, they were glad to accept the mission, especially when they heard how much money was involved.

Because he was interested in making an example of Clover Fields, the owner of the money that had been stuffed into her gym locker had offered a bounty equal to what was taken. He would pay for the pleasure and principle of maintaining his reputation, even if he didn't recover the money from the girl.

To a one percent club like the SBMC that was rarely invited to engage in money-generating activity without risk of jail time, the offer was exceptionally attractive.

"Just in case she can't pay back what she stole," he told Lock, "the client is going to get his money back some other way. So I'm not just needin' her alive. No marks."

Lock chuckled. "We'll treat her like blown glass."

"Do that very thing," Le Cocq said in punctuation, just to make it over abundantly clear that he wasn't kidding.

Within minutes Lock was martialing Stars and Bars. Every available member was expected to ride west in formation on a quest to nab a wanted girl worth fifty thousand fucking dollars.

CHAPTER FOURTEEN

THE DEVILS YOU KNOW

INXS – *Devil Inside*

T HE GAS TANK was almost full when Clover left
Dripping Springs, but by the time she got to
Channelview she practically had to coast into Buc-ee's
on fumes. She would have preferred a place that wasn't
so big and busy, but it was the only one that kept doors
to restroom and coffee open in the middle of the night.

She used the Ladies', drew an extra large extra bold
coffee, doused it with creamer, and grabbed snacks with
lots of sugar to help keep her awake. Just to be on the
safe side, she also bought four twenty-ounce Red Bulls
thinking that caffeine overdose couldn't be worse than
being turned over to a crime family that had inferred
her next stop would be the sex traffic auction block.

After setting the items in her arms and hands down on the cashier's counter, she said, "I also need to fill up and I'm paying cash."

"Okay," said the woman working the register. "How you doin' this evenin'?"

"Alright," Clover said, not feeling much like making new friends.

"That'll be seventeen twenty-three."

Clover handed over two ten dollar bills and got her change. "Okay. Can you turn on the pump on eight? Give me sixty dollars' worth?" She counted out another six ten-dollar bills and handed them over.

"Sure thing."

All the time she was pumping gas she was looking around for any indication that someone was overly interested in her. When the pump stopped, she quickly got behind the wheel. The tank was almost full. More than enough to get to Lafayette and figure out what to do next.

She turned the music up loud again knowing that high volume tunes and strong coffee was a good combination for staying alert.

As it happened, Stars and Bars member, Smoke Oakley, had been visiting a sister to see a brand new nephew in Baytown when he got the call that his MC was scouring the interstate corridor, west to east between Houston and Lafayette, looking for a girl in a Thin Lizzy tee. Like all Stars and Bars members, Smoke knew that route as well as his own name. Which wasn't really Smoke. Since bikes need to be fed every hundred and seventy-five miles or so, he was also familiar with the stops along the way and which ones were open for restrooms and food between midnight and six. Not many.

When you cut that number to just those on the eastbound side of the four lane, checking them out was doable. And the first one was right there in Baytown.

There were three cashiers working at Buc-ee's, which was lit up like midday.

He asked for a pack of smokes. "Hey, sweetheart."

The woman behind the counter smiled at the en-dearment. She wasn't the recipient of flirtation very often and Smoke was fairly good at it. He often quoted Bob Seger, "Ain't good lookin', but you know I ain't shy. Ain't afraid to look a girl in the eye."

He smiled. "I was supposed to meet my girlfriend down the road, but my phone's dead." He held up the back of his phone like he was submitting evidence, then quickly put it away in his pocket. "She might've stopped in here a little while ago. Real cute and wearin' a blue tee shirt. Bad Reputation on it?"

He knew by the way she blinked that he'd hit pay dirt. He remained outwardly calm, but was feeling like he'd won the lottery on the inside. His prez was going to see him in an entirely different light. The way he deserved to be seen. As vice-president material.

"Yeah. The red Jeep? Paid cash to fill it up about an hour or so ago."

He grinned at the lady. "Thanks, darlin'. You made my night."

She smiled.

He winked and turned on his heel. As soon as he was outside the building, he was dialing Lock.

"She's two hours from Lafayette, drivin' a red Jeep."

CLOVER HAD JUST passed a sign that said Lafayette thirty-two miles when she finished the last of her coffee. When she looked down to set the empty cup aside, she remembered the phone. Fishing in the oversized purse that sat on the passenger seat beside her, she found it and said, "Shit," when she saw there was a message.

She listened and hit call back.

"It's your phone," Brash said.

Raze took the phone, swiped to answer, and growled, "Why didn't you answer?"

"Sorry. I had the music turned up."

"Where are you?"

"I, um… why?"

"Why do you think? 'Cause I'm coming for you."

"You are not."

"Yes. I. Am."

She bit her bottom lip. Once it turned out that the shit fest wasn't going to go away as easy as it sounded the way Raze told it, she'd made a decision to keep him and his business out of it. Even if it meant taking her medicine.

It was evident that he liked her, but she didn't have any concrete reason to think he liked her enough to come after her.

"No. I'm leaving you out of this."

"Too late. I'm in it. So be a good girl and tell me where you are. Right now."

"I just passed a sign that said thirty-two miles to Lafayette."

"Okay. Gonna figure out a safe place for you to wait for me. Gonna call you back in a minute and tell you where. You gonna answer the phone when I call?"

She bit her bottom lip again. "Yes."

"Seems like you're a lot of trouble, stray girl."

"That's *exactly* why I want you out of this, Raze."

"Not an option. I'm countin' on you to pick up when I call you back."

"Okay."

"Is that a promise?"

"Yes. It's a promise."

He ended the call and handed the phone back to Brash. "I need a place where she can wait for us for... an hour if we keep makin' this time and don't get stopped."

Brash took the phone and called Brant who, in turn, called Just Batiste.

"She's a little less than half an hour out. Needs a place safe to wait for my people. What's open at this time of night and busy enough to discourage certain elements from drawing attention to themselves?"

"Waffle House on the south side. Exit Louisiana. Before she gets to Pont des Mouton. We'll keep people posted along I10. If we see her, yes, we'll give her an escort straight to our home. If no, at least ten of us will be waiting to bring her with us. I will personally drive her. Is she beautiful?"

"That is not funny."

Batiste laughed. "Joking. She is safe with Devils."

"Holdin' you to that. And, in case it's not understood. I owe you."

Batiste laughed. "Oh oui. Most *sure* was understood."

BRASH ANSWERED AS soon as the face of his phone lit, before it made a sound. "Yeah."

"Batiste says for her to go to the Waffle House. It's on I10 on the south side. Tell her to get off at Louisiana. The Devils have eyes on 10. If they see her and can catch her, they'll give her an escort to their facility. If not, there'll be at least ten waiting to take her to the club."

Brash relayed the information then dialed Raze's phone and handed it to him. When it rang three times, he said under his breath, "Come on. Make the right choice and pick the fuck up."

"Hello?" she said.

He closed his eyes with relief for as long as he dared while speeding along at ninety-two miles per hour.

"We have a plan. Go to the Waffle House. You're just twenty minutes away now. Probably. It'll be on your right. Get off at Louisiana. And now listen. 'Cause this is important. There are bikers out there, friends of ours, who are lookin' for you. If they see you before you get to the Waffle House, they'll try to overtake you and give you an escort. So don't be afraid. They're gonna take you to their club. You'll be safe till we get there. If they don't see you or don't catch you, there'll be others waitin' to take you to the club."

"Okay."

"You got all that?"

"Yes."

"I'm right here. If there's anything you're not sure about, call me."

"Okay."

"It's all gonna be okay."

She smiled in the darkness at his attempt to reassure. Raze was surprisingly nurturing for a wall of muscle, hard-edged biker-roadhouse owner. He couldn't see her smile, of course, but he did hear the big breath she took in, like she was summoning determination. Or courage. "Right. Later."

THIBAUT LE COCQ pulled into the Big T truck stop when he reached the first exit to Lafayette, and called the Stars and Bars prez.

"Lock," he answered. He was sitting on the deck of an Irish dive bar where he could keep an eye on his bike. It wasn't the kind of neighborhood where University of Louisiana Ragin' Cajuns were likely to go for off campus fun. But it was exactly the kind of place where Lock felt at home.

They were closed, of course. But it was as good a place as any to use as a half ass command center. He'd used the cutter he kept in his saddlebags to break the chain that kept deck chairs from disappearing overnight, pulled the top one off the stack and made himself comfortable.

"What've you got?"

Lock gave a low and humorless chuckle. "We might know somethin'. But you've given us fifty thousand spendable reasons not to share too early."

A muscle ticked in Thibaut's jaw. "Well. Let's amend the deal then. If you know where she is, let me in on it. I'll still honor the split. I'd rather see you with half than me with nothin'."

"Alright then," Lock drawled. "She should be pullin'

into the parish at any time now. Drivin' a red Jeep. I've got people posted on I10, keepin' an eye out. Don't know where she's headed, but we will pick her up and when we do, we won't lose her."

AFTER THE FIRST phone contact with Raze, Clover had slowed way down. Once she'd decided to stop blocking Raze's attempts to help, she reasoned that it made sense to slow down and give him a chance to catch up.

When she saw the first Lafayette exit, for Lafayette Parish and Acadia Parish, she decided to get off and go the rest of the way on the access road. That way she'd be sure to not miss the Waffle House. And since she wasn't in a big hurry…

While the Sons, the Stars, and the Devils all had people looking at I10, it was essentially impossible to spot a particular car. Headlights. Tail lights. Trucks. But picking out a particular SUV when most of the vehicles that were not trucks were SUVs? Unlikely at best.

So the plan to post eyes at the exits to Lafayette was a good one. The access roads were lit by street lights at the points of exits and vehicles had to slow or stop for traffic lights. That particular exit had a gas station convenience store on the northwest corner, another one just like it with a different name on the southwest corner, and a Whataburger on the southeast corner.

In the parking lot shadows of each of those enter-prises was a member of a motorcycle club, waiting idly but alert, watching for a red Jeep. None of the three were aware of the others until Stars and Bars roared in behind Clover as she slowed to stop at the red light.

Eric, from the SSMC, and the Cajun Devil, who'd illegally crossed four lanes and run a red light, pulled in behind Clover and the other biker. The two acknowl-edged each other with a nod. As they waited for the light, the Devil pulled out his phone, tapped it, and gave a hand signal he hoped would be understood, for his SSMC counterpart to call in the good news that they had the woman and the bad news that she had a Stars and Bars tail.

Eric did understand.

When the light changed, he went through then

pulled over and called Brant.

Aware of the other two bikers, Stars and Bars went around Clover, planning to stop at the next exit and call Lock with the news without losing sight of the Jeep.

"Boss," he said. "I got her on the access road, but we're not alone. Two other bikers are on us."

"WHAT OTHER BIKERS?" Lock stormed.

"Couldn't see their colors. You want me to stay on her or drop back and try to find out?"

Lock growled, "Stay on her." He ended the call and dialed up his VP who said, "Bunch of Devils were seen hanging out at the Waffle House. You think there's a connection?"

"Fuck. Yes. I think there's a connection."

Lock ended the call, but alerted every one of his guys to move toward the Waffle House. Since he was a suspicious son of a whore, he'd made every member in the club subscribe to Life 360 so that he could see where they were every minute of the day.

He got a fix on the bike following the target, stepped off the bar deck and threw a leg over his Harley. But there was one more thing to do before he headed over to see what the night would bring. He called Le Cocq. "You think you can find the Waffle House?"

CLOVER SLOWED AND stopped at the next light. Her headlights were shining directly on the Stars and Bars cut.

She dialed Raze.

He answered. "Here."

"I'm at a stop light on the access road. There's a biker in front of me. He's got one of those Confederate flag things on the back of his jacket. Is that who I'm supposed to go with?"

Raze's heart was starting to race and his breathing was getting heavier.

"What the hell is it?" Brash demanded.

"She's got Stars and Bars on her."

"Tell her to keep goin' to the Waffle House. Our people will be there."

"Alright. Listen sugar. Just keep goin' until you get to the Waffle House. Our people will be there. Cajun

Devils. Their colors look like a blue demon. Some or all of the Sons will probably be there, too. Don't worry. We've got you covered. Just don't pull over. No matter what. If he tries to force you over to the side of the road or make you stop, you just keep goin' even if you have to run over him and his bike. Your Jeep'll do that for you if you ask. When you get to the Waffle House, find the Devils and stay with them."

"Okay."

He hated the fact that her voice sounded shaky. She was there and he wasn't.

Brash called Brant as soon as he had the phone in his hand. Brant had already gotten the call from Eric and relayed the information to Batiste and Arnold, who was in charge of the SSMC arm of the operation until Brash was on the scene.

Within five minutes the members of all three clubs had been alerted that the vehicle of interest might be headed to the Waffle House.

Batiste called the sheriff, who was on speed dial, and woke him up.

"For the safely of your personnel, I strongly suggest you create a reason for them to be on the east side of town for the next couple of hours. All of them."

The sheriff sat up on the side of his bed. "Is this a situation that's going to come back on me?"

"Not if it can be avoided. But dead deputies will surely come back on you. Yes?"

"Christ. When?"

"Right now."

"Thanks for the heads up."

The parish sheriff's department was just a couple of blocks from the Waffle House. So the Devils had a front row seat to the spectacle of a parade of deputy vehicles racing away with lights flashing and sirens blasting.

Bikers from all three clubs took note of all the law enforcement vehicles racing west on the north I10 access road, away from where they were headed.

WHEN THE LIGHT changed, the biker in front of Clover moved forward and into the left lane. She was uncertain what to do, but continued in the right lane and passed him. Between an ignored red light and an extra burst of speed, Eric caught up with the Jeep.

Since Clover had picked up more bikers at every exit she passed, there were seven, counting Eric. Two Devils. Two Stars and Bars. Three SSMC.

She called Raze's phone again.

"I'm here," he answered.

"There are seven bikers behind me. I don't know whether they're your guys or…"

"Some of them are friends. You're probably close to the Waffle House. Just keep doin' what you're doin'. I'm almost there."

"Almost here? How can that be?"

"I, ah, drove fast."

"Oh. But why are they after me? If it was, um, taken care of?"

"Just a mix up. They said yes to the deal, but forgot to call off the dogs. By tomorrow it'll all be resolved. For good. Meantime, you're gonna be taken care of. Don't worry."

"Okay. I think I see a Waffle House sign."

"Look for the Devils. Some of us, I mean the SSMC, will be there, too."

"Uh-huh." She ended the call and put the phone in the drink holder.

The Waffle House sign was tall. Yellow with black block caps lettering.

The parking lot wasn't brightly lit, but there was enough illumination to make out the twenty-five or so bikes parked at the north end. She drove straight toward them and stopped, shining her lights directly into the faces of the men who were standing around, some of them smoking. She thought she recognized some of them from Bike Night at the roadhouse, but wasn't taking any chances.

The biker who'd been following on the access road turned into the Waffle House parking lot entrance, but fell back and joined a few other bikers.

After a few seconds of keeping her headlights trained on the bikers in front of her, a couple of them came forward. One was a youngish heartthrob. Black hair, blue eyes, and a cocky smile. The other was a guy she was pretty sure she'd seen at the roadhouse earlier that very same night, which seemed liked it was weeks in the past.

The pretty one tapped his knuckles on her window. She shook her head and said, "Turn around," through the glass.

Batiste complied, as did the other guy.

There was the blue demon Raze had said to look for and the temple snake she'd seen the SSMC bikers wear. She rolled down the window.

"I'm Clover," she said.

"Clover." Batiste smiled. "Can you move to the other side of the car and let me drive?"

She nodded.

When he got in and started the car, everybody got on their bikes, readying to ride out. But when he turned toward the exit, a white van pulled in followed by the deafening noise of twenty-two motorcycles who formed a blockade in front of the exit.

"Huh," Batiste said, absent of the concern most people would think appropriate for the circumstance.

"Seems there will be a delay in our departure."

He smiled at Clover in a way that would normally accompany something like an announcement that dessert was being served.

The bikers who had straddled their bikes dismounted as Batiste backed the Jeep up.

It was a standoff.

Twenty-two Stars and Bars with whatever was inside that white van.

Twenty-five combined Devils and SSMC, one red Jeep.

And the girl that everybody there was determined to leave with.

The Devils' prez had sent somebody inside to confiscate phones and assure the occupants of the building that no one would be harmed. As it was four on a Friday morning, or a Thursday night depending on your point of view, there were only four people present. A cook. A waitress. And a road-weary couple moving their stuff in a U-Haul truck from Jackson to New Orleans.

The cook, who was in his late sixties, but had once been a biker, took it in stride and offered the Devil something to eat. He smiled and asked the cook, "You got a landline in here?"

The cook nodded and led the way. The Devil unplugged the phone and took it along with the four cell phones. "I'll bring these back shortly. If you'd just make sure everybody stays calm. When I return the phones, there'll be a good tip for you and a free dinner for the nice couple."

BATISTE GOT OUT of the Jeep, walked a few feet forward, and raised his voice. "It's your intention to prevent us from leaving?"

The driver's door of the white van opened. A guy in collared polo, jeans, boots, and a baseball cap got out with a bullhorn.

"My business is with the lady," he said, the bullhorn boosting his voice like an amped mic. "Clover Fields. Look around you. There are a lot of people here who could get hurt. I know you don't want that. You're a

VICTORIA DANANN

receptionist. Not a desperado. So come on over here and go with me peacefully. You won't be harmed and neither will any of these people."

For a few seconds the only sound was the whirr of an eighteen-wheeler passing by on the interstate. She opened the passenger door and got out.

"No," Arnold said as he marched toward her planning to physically put her back in the car and close the door.

She read all of that in his face and knew she had only a fraction of a second to make her decision. She chose Raze. She knew he was close, which made him vulnerable to whatever was about to happen as well as his friends. And for what? To save her from what she probably deserved.

Because, in truth, when she was brutally honest with herself, she knew that money wasn't hers and that she shouldn't be paying off her debts with it. Certainly other people shouldn't have to pay for that mistake just because they loved somebody who wanted to protect her.

All that processed in the lightning-fast computer that is the human brain in an instant and before Arnold could reach her she ran straight toward Thibaut Le Cocq, whose expression changed to pure shock.

He'd thought the bullhorn thing was worth a shot, but he wouldn't have given it hundred to one odds to work. He gaped as she ran toward him. What Clover didn't know was that the SSMC and Devils were right behind her. They were slowed down by surprise, biker boots, and the fact that none of them had been all city high school sprinters just four years earlier as she had.

When she came within grabbing distance, Le Cocq turned her around and took her into a neck hold and put a gun to her head. "Here's what we're about to do. None of you gentlemen will move till I secure my prisoner."

He began to drag Clover backward toward the rear of the van when a Dodge truck came practically flying over the curb and across the landscaping, snapping the steel cables that held Brash's bike in place so that it tipped over.

When the pickup came to a rest as if it was tailgating the faceoff, Raze slammed open his door and rushed toward Clover, but stopped dead when he saw the gun to her head.

HE'D FORGOTTEN ABOUT Bless, who understood everything about Clover being in danger and understood nothing about guns. While Brash was getting out of the truck, Bless squeezed between the seats, leaped from the open driver's side door, and charged the bounty hunter.

When he saw ninety-four pounds of canine streaking toward him, he loosened his hold on Clover and moved the gun to aim at the dog.

She took in what was happening as if it was in slow motion and when she saw the gun muzzle move so that it was pointed at Bless, she screamed, "NO!" and threw her entire weight toward the arm that held the gun. Le Cocq's trigger finger squeezed involuntarily, but he fired in the direction of Raze's truck and hit no one.

Bless was unconcerned with everything except sinking her teeth into Le Cocq and holding on.

If the Stars and Bars had had their wits about them, they would have prevented Clover from leaving, but they were caught up in the surprise and drama of an enraged German Shepherd and stray gunfire. So she slipped away easily and ran to Raze who opened his arms for her at the same time he shouted, "Ostenov-livalivatseeya!"

Bless had Le Cocq on the ground, curled into a ball, whimpering, and trying to protect his face and neck with his arms.

The dog's vicious snarls stopped as quickly and completely as if she'd been unplugged. She trotted over to Raze and looked up, wagging her tail, with Le Cocq's blood all over her face.

"Good girl," Raze said, reaching down to give her a heartfelt petting.

LOCK TOOK A look at Le Cocq on the ground. Even if they fought the Devils *and* the SSMC for the girl, they weren't going to get their money. He spat on the ground.

"Let's go," he said.

Within two minutes the Stars and Bars were headed east on I10, leaving Le Cocq where he fell. *Fucker.*

Phones were returned to Waffle House personnel and patrons. And an invitation was extended to the SSMC to use the Devils' guest rooms for some sleep and have a genuine Cajun breakfast.

They thanked the Devils, said they'd chug energy drinks instead.

"Brant says to call him tomorrow," Brash told Batiste. "We're ready to sign some papers."

Batiste grinned and shook Brash's hand enthusiastically. "You could do worse than us for friends."

"After tonight, don't see how we can argue with that," Brash said. Witnessing that the Devils were willing to stand for a fire fight for no other reason than being asked was an actions-speak-louder-than-words event.

RAZE WAS STILL feeling adrenaline pumping through his veins. Seeing Clover with a gun at her head had scared him more than anything he'd *ever* experienced. And considering his history, that was saying something.

He wrapped her up tight in his arms and squeezed until every cell in his brain and body was convinced she was alright. When he loosened his hold, he said in a raspy voice, "You saved my dog."

Clover's arms still encircled his waist. She dropped her head back so she could see his face. "No. The dog saved me."

Raze smiled and kissed her on the forehead. "Know one thing. Anybody who tries to fuck with my girls is gonna be sorry."

IT TOOK FOUR guys to stand Brash's bike back up and get it out of the truck, but it was rideable.

"Gotta love Harley Davidson." Brash laughed.

So they changed the tire on Raze's truck. They put Dev's bike in the truck and he drove it back because Brash was more than ready to be out in the open. Not to mention that he expected Raze and Clover might like some time alone.

Before they left Brash asked Raze, "When did you learn the special commands?"

"Rescue taught 'em to me. I didn't think I'd ever need them, but it turned out it was a good idea. The Russian thing's kind of genius."

"Yeah. Rescue's one of a kind."

Brash turned away to call Brant and debrief. "Damnedest thing. There are fifty badass bikers standin' around watchin' the girl and the dog take care of business. Never heard of anything like it." He laughed.

WHEN BRASH ENDED the call to Brant, Raze and Clover were getting ready to leave. They'd argued about who was going to drive until they finally resolved it with a coin toss. Raze won. He said he'd drive the first two hours and give the wheel to her with no intention of doing so.

Brash caught the passenger door of the Jeep as Clover was getting in. In a hushed tone that only she could hear, he said, "You'd better not break his heart."

Clover took in the serious expression on Brash's

handsome face. As he closed the door, she made no reply, but thought how glad she was that Raze had friends who loved him.

TRAVELING ON I10 at a reasonable speed, the sun coming up behind them, Raze said, "So you got no reason to be going anywhere now."

After a few minutes she said, "I do have a reason. A big one. I owe you a truckload of money. If things are really going to be settled, the smart thing would be to find the best paying job I can get so I can pay you back before time to worry about how I'm going to pay for the nursing home. I'm not complaining about tips, but it will take most of my life to pay you back at that rate."

"That'd be the smart thing to do?"

"Yes. I think so."

"You do *not* think that would be the smart thing to do."

"I don't?"

"No. The smart thing would be to accept that the debt's paid. You don't owe me anything. But the rest of your life."

She laughed. "Is that a joke?"

He didn't look like he was kidding. "No, stray girl. It's not a joke. We got somethin' between you and me. You know that. Right?"

"Of course I know there's a… spark. Maybe I could stick around long enough to find out if it goes somewhere?"

Raze was shaking his head. "No. We're not lookin' at things that way."

"We're not?"

"No."

"How are we looking at things?"

"Like this. I'm gonna be your family. You're gonna be mine. I'm gonna be your best friend. You're gonna be mine. Every night I'm goin' to sleep thanking all that's holy that you're in my bed. Every morning I'm wakin' up thanking all that's holy that you're in my arms and I'm gonna remind myself that there could never be another woman 'cause nobody's as cute and cuddly as you." At that point Clover felt her eyes stinging and knew he was seeing the telltale signs of tearing up, but she was powerless to stop the emotion from rising.

She was liking what she was hearing.

So. Much.

But he wasn't yet done.

"And you're gonna wake up every mornin' knowing that there could never be another man 'cause nobody's gonna care for you and protect you and appreciate you the way I do." The first tear spilled over her bottom lashes and ran down her cheek. He reached over and wiped it away with his thumb. "What's that about?"

"You're talking commitment."

He cocked his head. "Glad to see you're up to speed."

She smiled and swiped at her face. "We barely know each other."

"Bullshit. We know enough. We know we fit and what else is there?"

"What else is there?" she repeated then shook her head. "Nothing else matters."

He slowed then pulled off on the side of the road before treating her to his grin that was both sardonic and spectacular. The one that made her forget to breathe. It was sexy. It was joyful. It was glorious in the way of brightening everything within her visual perimeter. Her lips parted in appreciation just before he took advantage of that by delivering a deep kiss of claiming, one she would still remember when she was a nonagenarian.

When she recovered her wits, she said, "In that case, I think I should ask about your name. What is it?"

"Raze."

She rolled her eyes and gave him a look. "The name on your birth certificate."

He sighed deeply, looked away, but seemed to make up his mind that he'd tell her anything she wanted to know. "Leif."

She laughed. "Come on. What is it really?"

He chuckled, shaking his head. "Darlin'. I'm not that clever. Swear to Christ, it's Leif."

She studied him until she came to believe he might

be telling the truth. "Well then. It's a sign."

"What kinda sign?"

"That we're destined to be together."

He laughed. Raze didn't know about signs or destiny or the like. He didn't believe in soul mates or falling in love at first sight or any crap like that. But he did believe that there was an adorably quirky blonde who'd sewn up the wounds and filled up the holes and made life look like something worth doing again.

As Raze relived the events of the night a question came up in his mind. "How'd he get ahold of you anyway?"

She sighed. "He said your friends were going to get hurt if I didn't go with him." She fiddled with the hem of her shirt. "I couldn't let that happen. I mean, I did take the money." She turned to look out the window at the landscapes she hadn't seen in the dark of night.

"You mean the SSMC and the Devils just let you walk off? Into the hands of a bounty hunter?" He sounded incredulous.

"Well, they didn't exactly *let* me. I kind of ran before they had a chance to figure out I was going. I was a sprinter in high school." She giggled. "Guess I've still got it."

"You're full of surprises, aren't ya?" She shrugged prettily. "Yeah. And you're plenty cute, too. But don't ever think about doin' somethin' so half-witted again." She opened her mouth to protest, but he had more to say. "So far as the money goes, you seem to have a cockeyed view of morality."

"Oh really."

"Yeah. You didn't steal money from somebody else's gym locker. Did you?"

"No."

"That's right. It was *your* locker. Somebody put a pile of ill-gotten gains in *your* locker. So far as you were concerned it was a bird nest on the ground. You know why you thought that?"

"Why?"

"Because on some level you knew the lockers all around yours were rented by women who weren't storing three hundred thousand dollars of cash in duffels."

"Two seventy five."

"Whatever. You also knew somebody had to pick your lock to get in. Right?"

"Yes. But honestly, I did know it wasn't mine."

He laughed. "That's just it, sugar. It wasn't theirs either."

She sat back, cocked her head and thought about that. Raze might have used machinations to come to his conclusion, but it was logical. "I didn't do anything wrong."

"Now she's getting' it. You didn't do anything wrong except put your sweet self in danger. Which you are *never* gonna do again. Right?"

She grinned. "Right."

He really, really, really wanted to believe her. But it didn't matter. If she was one of those people who had trouble trailing her around, she was still his. Right or wrong. Good or bad.

"Just saying though." She looked at her nails. "That women who are fast can do what they want."

EPILOGUE

"**C**LOVER!" LUKE YELLED from the other end of the bar. "He says to get home now. Puppies are comin'."

"Eek." She squealed, threw her apron on the bar and ran toward the door.

Bless gave birth to seven precious black bundles of fur. Clover cried during the entire birth, swearing to Bless that they were keeping them all, while Raze was contradicting every one of those promises.

"Will you stop telling her that? We're not havin' seven German Shepherd dogs."

"Why not?"

"'Cause we need to save room and time for kids."

"We're having kids?"

"I thought we would."

"Raze. We're not married."

"We're promised. Same thing."

"No. It's not."

"Is to me."

"Well, it's not to me."

Raze barked out a laugh. "Swore I'd never get married again."

"Yes, well, me, too. But *you're* not *him*!"

He shook his head smiling, eyes lit with amusement. "That's a fact."

Clover narrowed her eyes. "And I'm not *her!*"

Raze's smile fell away as his features sobered. He locked her gaze as if to punctuate that he was serious. "That is *also* a fact."

"And stupid ass vows are made to be broken." After a brief pause, she said, "*And* you need to stop calling me 'stray girl' because I'm not a stray. I belong here."

He smiled broadly. "You don't?"

She huffed.

He walked out of the room without another word and Clover turned her attention back to the puppies.

"You're the best mother in the world, Bless. Look how gorgeous and perfect your babies are. They're so sweet and they smell so good. They're like heaven with little soft paws."

Bless was lying on her side, but moved her head just enough so that Clover would know she was aware that Clover was talking to her.

The sound of Raze's boots scuffing back into the kitchen was followed by him standing over her, saying, "So will you?"

"Will I what?" She'd shifted her focus to the pure pleasure of German Shepherd babies and pretty much forgotten about the topic of discussion from just a few minutes before.

"Jesus. You're really gonna make me do it, aren't ya?"

She turned around to look at him, but since she was sitting on the floor, when he went to one knee she was still looking up at him.

He held out the most spectacular diamond marquis ring she'd ever seen. And he knew he'd gotten it right when he heard her little feminine gasp.

"Will you marry me?"

She got to her knees, threw herself into his arms, and planted playful kisses all over his face.

"That's a yes, then."

"I already agreed to be 'ruined' forever. But who doesn't love a party? We are having a party, right?"

"What's the point of owning a roadhouse if we can't throw a party for our own wedding?"

"Exactly." She laughed and gave him three rapid fire kisses with her arms thrown around his neck. "And I like the ring. A lot."

He tilted his head back so that he was looking through amused and partially hooded eyes. "How much?"

"Enough to try that thing."

"That thing?" He smiled. "The thing that makes you blush and hide your face." She nodded. He chuckled. "I'm glad you like the ring. But you like me best. Right?"

"I like you better than all the other wonderful things in life put together."

"Hmmm. Almost sounds like this thing I heard of."

"What?"

"Love."

She searched his eyes. "Does sound like that, doesn't it?"

"Is that how you feel about me?"

"Is that how you feel about me?" she countered.

"I think maybe since the second I looked up and saw a stray girl wander into my roadhouse."

"Say it."

He planted a kiss on her lips and said, "I love you," without pulling away.

She giggled. "It's so weird that the best thing I ever did was steal money from criminals."

NEXT UP IN MC ROMANCE

Batiste, the first book of the Cajun Devils MC series.

I sincerely hope you enjoyed reading *Roadhouse*.

Reviews are enormously helpful to me. Please take the time to follow a link back to the book you've just read and post your thoughts. A few words are often as powerful as many.

Victoria Danann NEW YORK TIMES and USA TODAY BESTSELLING AUTHOR

For no-more-than-once-a-month news/releases **text VICTORIA** (in all caps) to **67076**.

SUBSCRIBE TO MY PODCAST Romance Between the Pages

www.romancecast.com

(Personal interviews with the biggest names in romance, every Friday.)

Victoria's Website LINKS TO ALL Victoria's books can be found here!

www.victoriadanann.com

Victoria's Facebook Page

facebook.com/victoriadanannbooks

Victoria's Facebook Fan Group

facebook.com/groups/772083312865721

Twitter

twitter.com/vdanann

Pinterest

pinterest.com/vdanann

Also by Victoria Danann

CONTEMPORARY ROMANCE

SSMC Austin, TX, Book 1. Two Princes

SSMC Austin, TX, Book 2. The Biker's Brother

SSMC Austin, TX, Book 3. Nomad

SSMC Austin, TX, Book 4. Devil's Marker

SSMC Austin, TX, Book 5. Roadhouse

Cajun Devils Book 1. Batiste

THE KNIGHTS OF BLACK SWAN

Knights of Black Swan 1. My Familiar Stranger

Knights of Black Swan 2. The Witch's Draam

Knights of Black Swan 3. A Summoner's Tale

Knights of Black Swan 4. Moonlight

Knights of Black Swan 5. Gathering Storm

Knights of Black Swan 6. A Tale of Two Kingdoms

Knights of Black Swan 7. Solomon's Sieve

Knights of Black Swan 8. Vampire Hunter

Knights of Black Swan 9. Journey Man

Knights of Black Swan 10. Falcon

Knights of Black Swan 11. Jax

Knights of Black Swan 12. Deliverance

ORDER OF THE BLACK SWAN D.I.T.

D.I.T. 1. Simon Says

D.I.T. 2. Finngarick

D.I.T. 3. Irish War Cry

ORDER OF THE BLACK SWAN NOVELS

Black Swan Novel, Prince of Demons

THE HYBRIDS

Exiled 1. CARNAL

Exiled 2. CRAVE

Exiled 3. CHARMING

THE WEREWOLVES

New Scotia Pack 1. Shield Wolf: Liulf

New Scotia Pack 2. Wolf Lover: Konochur

New Scotia Pack 3. Fire Wolf: Cinaed

THE WITCHES OF WIMBERLEY

Made in the USA
Columbia, SC
27 May 2018